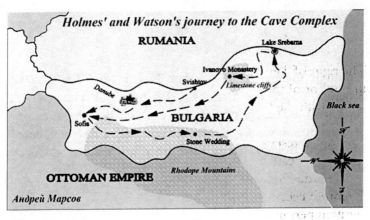

Holmes' and Watson's journey to the Cave Complex

RUMANIA

Lake Srebarna

Ivanovo Monastery

Svishtov

Limestone cliffs

Danube

Black sea

Sofia

BULGARIA

Stone Wedding

OTTOMAN EMPIRE

Rhodope Mountains

Андрей Марсов

Although the events in *Sherlock Holmes And The Case Of The Bulgarian Codex* are fictional, the principal character Prince Ferdinand is based closely on one of the most compelling personalities in world history, the real Prince Regnant, later Tsar, who ruled Bulgaria from 1887 until his forcible abdication in 1918.

TO MY BEAUTIFUL PARTNER LESLEY ABDELA

Nargakot, Nepal. Photo Lesley Abdela

Tim Symonds was born in London. He grew up in Somerset, Dorset and Guernsey. After several years in East and Central Africa he settled in California and graduated Phi Beta Kappa in Political Science from UCLA. He is a Fellow of the Royal Geographical Society. Like his first novel, *Sherlock Holmes And The Dead Boer At Scotney Castle* (MX Publishing 2012), he wrote *The Case of The Bulgarian Codex* in the woods and remote valleys surrounding his home in the High Weald of East Sussex. More than a century ago, Sherlock Holmes's creator explored the same woodlands from his favourite base at the Ashdown Forest Hotel in the run-up to his second marriage. In *The Adventure of Black Peter* Conan Doyle has Dr. Watson remark admiringly, 'the Weald was once part of that great forest which for so long held the Saxon invaders at bay'.

CONTENTS

CHAPTER I
IN WHICH WE DINE AT SIMPSON'S

SNORTING and champing at the bit like a high-strung warhorse, the Orient Express stayed its departure from the Gare de Strasbourg while Sherlock Holmes and I flung ourselves from a five-glass landau and clambered into the private cars of the Prince Regnant of Bulgaria. Our boxes tumbled in behind us. It was late on a Friday afternoon in April, in the year 1900. The case of the Bulgarian Codex had commenced. With a minatory scream the immense train pulled away on its long journey to Stamboul. Soon Paris was left behind. Without noise or jerk we were going fifty miles per hour without seeming to move.

Hardly two days earlier we found a visitor of European fame within the walls of our humble room in Baker Street, a being so utterly unusual in personality and mentality that I remember him in precise detail to this day, despite the passage of many chaotic and adventurous years.

I was seated at my writing-desk at 221B Baker Street putting the final touches to our most recent case for the *Strand Magazine*, with no more a thought about a fractious Balkan state than for the industrious navigators repairing the canals of Mars. The winter, never severe in the centre of London, was on the cusp of a warm and exhilarating spring. I looked across the garden to the back wall which leads into Mortimer Street. More than once, in fear of attack from Baker Street, Holmes and I made a quick exit by that route. Observing the unfurling leaves on the mighty London planes it was impossible to know we would soon be risking life and limb in a faraway country about which I—and most of the civilised world—knew or cared nothing. By early afternoon I would finish the manuscript, throw my pen at the wall as was my custom on completing each new chronicle, and take a comfortable stroll to the editor's offices on Southampton Street. It would then be up to the *Strand's* Art editor to commission a few simple line drawings from the established artist Mr. Sidney Paget.

Holmes came up the stairs at his customary three-at-a-time. He put his head around the door, a Coutts cheque flapping in his hand.

'My dear Watson,' he said in a most affable tone. 'Courtesy of the mid-day post, the Duchess of Timau has at last settled her account. Name any restaurant in the whole of London and allow me to invite you to dine there this evening. Shall we say a fish-dinner at The Ship, in Greenwich?'

The invitation came as a welcome surprise. When fortune smiles on me I will lay out two days' Army pension on partridge or an over-ripe pheasant at one of my clubs, or, for a special treat, Rother Rabbit with broccoli followed by Lady Pettus' biscakes. Holmes, by contrast, even when he is the honoured guest of a wealthy client, has been known to call for a tin of his favourite over-salted Benitez corned beef.

'Holmes, I accept this rare invitation,' I replied, and added, 'with alacrity.'

'And if not The Ship, the place for our celebratory meal?' Holmes pursued.

'If you really do mean any restaurant in the whole of London I shall choose Simpson's Grand Cigar Divan.'

'A fine choice,' Holmes acknowledged cheerily.

At seven o' clock that evening, Simpson's head waiter led us to a table overlooking the Strand. The window commanded a fine sweep of the Vaudeville and Strand theatres, busy beyond measure. Many famous men had sat here, not least Gladstone and most of the greatest authors of our time. Each Feast of All Souls, Charles Dickens booked this same table with fellow members of the Everlasting Club to discuss the occult, Egyptian magic and second sight.

We selected our meal from the superb bill of fare. After a suitable time the Chef appeared, walking imposingly alongside the lesser mortal propelling a silver dinner wagon. Holmes ordered slices of beef carved from large joints, with a due portion of fat. At a price well beyond my usual range, I partook of the smoked salmon, a signature dish of the establishment. For dessert, we chose the Grand Cigar Divan's famous treacle sponge with a dressing of Madagascan vanilla custard.

As we progressed, Holmes's mood became pensive. I enquired. He responded with a sigh.

'Watson, I pine for change. While you attend to the Dark Arts, writing your chronicles, I sit in desolation waiting for the next ring of the door-bell. Our adventures of late have been somewhat parochial, summoned hither and thither to one or other *bijou* villa in a London suburb or English village. My study of chemistry and a new combination of gases is not enough. I am in the mood for something more exotic.'

'Perhaps it is the effect of a new Century or this wonderful spring weather?' I offered. 'The season of unrest and change. It makes all Nature restless.'

'Think what events are taking place elsewhere while we live out our tidy lives in Baker Street,' my fellow-lodger went on, unheeding. 'In Paris and Vienna it is the era of the Rothschilds, of brilliant cotillions and *tableaux vivants*. The Strausses conduct orchestras at Court balls. And ballooning—ballooning is becoming the fashion. Even that court actress, Katharina Schratt, has made three ascents.'

Although on the present occasion he was in a black sack coat and stiff collar, and looked eminently respectable, to listen to our landlady's sighs as she dusted and brushed and wiped at such knick-knacks as a huge barbed-headed spear, a bear's skull, a wall-plaque of the great Jewish fighter Dan Mendoza, rated by Holmes as the Father of the pugilistic science, a carving of the demi-god Maui, a harpoon engraved SS SEA UNICORN Dundee, a pair of seal's paws and the tennis rackets and cricket gear he last employed in his short time at Oxford and Cambridge, tidy was not the word I would have used to describe Holmes's life. Not even the large, cracked blue-and-white plate looted at the siege of Alexandria in 1882 by the son of one of my elderly patients or the butter-dish was immune from the residues of his chemical experiments.

'Holmes,' I began, laying down my napkin with a smile. 'Surely you cannot be bored so soon? The greatest figures of our time welcome you to their tables. Only a fortnight has passed since you solved the case I shall title *The Adventure of the Tall Man*. How you deduced the imprints below the window were from stilts and not the legs of a ladder still escapes me.'

'Watson, I value your effort to console me with my notoriety but I insist that every morning one must win a victory and every evening we must fight the good fight to retain our place. The crisis once over, the actors pass for ever out of our lives. For the moment the future seems more than unusually uncertain.'

To cheer him I responded, 'Who knows when the next knock at our door or telegram will come, summoning us to the scene of another baffling crime?'

A small tureen sitting apart from the magnificent silverware on our table came to Holmes's attention. We summoned the waiter. With the utmost earnestness he said he knew nothing about it. I pulled the tureen towards me and lifted the cover.

Inside lay an envelope marked 'Sherlock Holmes, Esq.'. It contained a sheet of pink-tinted note-paper upon which, in a scribbled hand, were inscribed the words: 'I shall come to your premises at five o' clock on matters of an importance which can hardly be exaggerated.'

I passed the note to Holmes. 'Our recent successes have made us incautious,' he remarked ruefully. 'That tureen could as easily have served up a parboiled swamp adder.' In a satisfied tone, he added, 'Yet I deduce that the man who sent it is an opportunist, not an enemy with threats on our person in mind. To judge by the peremptory message he is accustomed to having his own way. And this note-paper. He is a man of some means. Such paper could not be bought under half a crown a packet.'

He returned the page to me. 'See how peculiarly strong and stiff it is. Look at the watermark,' he continued. 'It is not an English paper at all. Your encouraging words may be coming true.'

CHAPTER II
IN WHICH WE MEET A ROYAL PERSONAGE

BACK at our Baker Street lodgings, having dined, wined, and conversed at Simpson's to a most heart-warming degree, I went to my bed leaving Holmes stooping over a retort and a test-tube. I fell at once into a peaceful sleep. It seemed hardly a minute passed before I awoke to a tapping at my door. Holmes was calling to me in a low urgent tone.

'Watson, if you can spare the time I should be very glad of your company.'

It was pitch black. Only very gradually my misty brain took the words in.

I peered in the direction of the voice. 'Holmes,' I balked, 'are we on fire?' I struck a match and looked at my watch. 'Heavens, my dear fellow, it's half past four in the morning!'

'Join me at our windows in ten minutes,' came the reply. 'I remind you our prospective client promised to arrive at five o' clock.'

'Whoever left the letter for us surely meant the more civilised hour of five in the afternoon!' I protested.

'My friend,' came the amused reply, 'no-one who commands Ariel to deliver his messages would come to our lodgings at five in the afternoon! At that hour half the world is out and about on Baker Street. A vital wish for privacy must bring our client here under the cover of a moonless night.'

I had hardly joined my fellow-lodger by a newly-lighted fire before his hand shot up. He glanced at me like a Baluchi hound. 'Hark! If I am not mistaken, our man arrives early. *L'exactitude est la politesse des rois.* A motorised barouche is about to halt at our door.'

Galvanised, we hurried to a window and parted the blinds. A taxi, a Panhard-Levassor landaulet, approached the kerb, the folding top raised against a blustery shower. Even before the vehicle came to a stop the kerb-side door swung open. A remarkable apparition emerged.

It was not the man's height, though considerable, which caught my immediate attention but his extraordinary attire. A black vizard mask concealed the upper part of his face, extending down past the cheekbones. Heavy bands of black astrakhan were slashed across the sleeves and fronts of a double-breasted coat. An Egyptian-blue cloak lined with flame-coloured silk was thrown over his shoulders. Boots extended halfway up his calves, trimmed at the tops with rich brown fur, completing a deliberate impression of barbaric opulence.

Readers may be familiar with *A Scandal in Bohemia*, the first of our cases published in the *Strand*, where a Royal personage clad in identical fashion sprang upon us in our modest lodgings like a puma launching from a Brazil Nut tree in the Mato Grosso.

A Scandal In Bohemia remains a cherished memory. I am reminded of the chronicle by the occasional glimpse of a magnificent snuffbox of old gold, with a great amethyst in the centre of the lid, presented to Holmes by the King.

'Holmes,' I exclaimed. 'The Hereditary King of Bohemia has returned!'

My companion took his eyes from the Panhard-Levassor landaulet and gave a mocking laugh. 'Watson, how well this story festers in the back of your cerebellum! While he is undoubtedly tall, our present visitor cannot be more than six feet one inch in height, whereas the King of Bohemia was hardly less than six feet six inches, with the chest and limbs of a Hercules. Clearly our visitor is acquainted with your chronicles. I suspect he has more on his mind than this masquerade if he has persisted in coming to our door in an April storm.'

While Holmes spoke, a short exchange was taking place between our startled landlady and the visitor. We fell back into our chairs by the fire.

Mrs. Hudson's familiar knock was followed by the door flying open. The apparition strode in, the cloak secured at the neck with a *cameo habille*, the carved woman's neck adorned by a tiny diamond necklace. To Mrs. Hudson's discomfit, with a quick placement of a hand the stranger turned her quickly around, pressing the door shut behind her.

I sprang out of my chair.

'Why, Holmes,' I gasped, pointing towards our visitor in mock surprise, 'I do declare it is none other than the Hereditary King of Bohemia who honours us once again.'

Our visitor tore off the mask, waving aside my offer of brandy. Beneath fair, wavy hair in perfect order and fine, high brows, another notable feature delineated his face: a majestic pair of mustachios, extravagant in their length and curl. He looked down at the still-seated Holmes through narrow eyes.

'Not quite the King of Bohemia, Dr. Watson,' our visitor returned. 'No, not the dear Wilhelm Gottsreich Sigismond von Ormstein, as I see our Mr. Holmes has already deduced,' he continued, 'or surely he would have rushed to greet an old client.'

The voice, though nasal, was decisive.

He continued, 'Yet the matter is so delicate that like the King of Bohemia I dare not confide it to an agent without putting myself in the man's power. I have come incognito from Sofia for the purpose of consulting you. I am Ferdinand, Prince Regnant of Bulgaria. I require your services. I require them immediately. It concerns a matter of the utmost discretion and importance.'

'Bulgaria?' I enquired.

'Yes, Dr. Watson. Surely you have heard of Bulgaria, the tinderbox of Europe? A land of mystery, mosques and minarets, all the faces of mankind—Kurds, Druze, Jews, Ismailis— wonderfully mixed?'

He paused, staring at me quizzically.

I remained silent. He added, 'Men in fezzes and baggy knickerbockers who carry old-fashioned firearms and curved knives stuck in their belts? My Capital Sofia throngs with stout Persian merchants, wild Turcomans, Parsees from Bombay and Hebrew rabbis by the dozen, even children of the Land of the Dragon. Your public must thirst to know of such strange and mountainous lands. Look how the English feast on such things:

I met a traveller from an antique land
Who said: Two vast and trunkless legs of stone
Stand in the desert. Near them, on the sand,
Half sunk, a shattered visage lies, whose frown,
And wrinkled lip, and sneer of cold command,'

and so on.'

He put a hand across his face, peering at me through his fingers. 'Veiled women with enchanting eyes; men in jackets of crimson velvet embroidered with gold or silver, riding spirited Arab steeds whose hooves strike sparks on the *kaldrmi*. Bazaars the equal of Baghdad's. Abracadabra! You will be able to regale your readers with adventures and discoveries as picturesque as the *One Thousand And One Nights*.'

I gestured at his attire. 'But, I beg you, how were you able to—?'

'—adopt the disguise of another Royal visitor of yours? My dear Dr. Watson, I do not just read your chronicles, I devour them like the bear fishing in a river's rapids, sinking its teeth into a writhing salmon. I learn your stories by rote, word for word. They are issued as a text-book to the Bulgarian police-force. However, I assure you that on this occasion you will not be required to regain an unseemly picture of me and the late Irene Adler, of dubious and questionable memory, such as the photograph you refer to in *A Scandal in Bohemia*.'

Holmes half opened his lids and glanced across at our visitor. 'You say you require our services—?' He broke off, reaching for his briar pipe.

Our strange visitor stretched beneath his cloak and withdrew a heavy chamois leather bag. He let it drop on the table.

'This bag contains exactly three hundred pounds in sovereigns and seven hundred in notes,' he said, 'plus a few dozen Bulgarian gold 100 *leva* bearing my head—for your expenses in my country. Accept this as a mark of my esteem.'

He added, 'You would not expect the Prince Regnant of Bulgaria to pay you any less than the King of Bohemia!'

I stared mesmerised at the bulky leather bag.

'Your Royal Highness,' I returned. 'That is a very generous sum. We must assume the matter is of the highest importance.'

Our visitor seated himself on the sofa.

'Important enough to bring a Prince out in such a gale,' he answered.

Our visitor followed this with a backward glance at the door. He turned to Sherlock Holmes and murmured 'Mr. Holmes, if I am to explain exactly why there is nothing of greater importance to the entire world than the commission I am about to proffer, I must presume I have your utmost assurance of confidentiality?'

Holmes reassured him with a 'You may'; adding with a gesture in my direction, 'Your Highness, I undertake nothing serious without my trusted comrade and biographer at my elbow.'

'Importance to the *entire world*?' I could not prevent myself asking.

The Prince's forehead wrinkled at my incredulous response.

'To the entire world,' he repeated impatiently. 'It concerns the loss of a centuries-old manuscript known as the Codex Zographensis, the most ancient and most sacred manuscript in the Old Bulgarian language. Since the news came that it has been taken from a hiding-place believed to be completely secure I have hardly had a wink of sleep.'

'Let us hear more of this Codex Zographensis,' Holmes broke in. 'Why is its loss of such importance? Why would you come all the way from Sofia by way of Simpson's Grand Cigar Divan to our quarters at this hour, and in the teeth of our famous weather?'

'The Codex is an illuminated manuscript, a gospel-book more than a thousand years old,' our guest related. 'For many centuries it was believed lost or destroyed. Sixty years ago it was rediscovered at the Zograf Monastery on Mount Athos and found its way back to Bulgaria. From the moment of its return the Codex took on a mystical importance, a talisman of national destiny, like the Golden Throne of the Ashanti, or the Stone of Scone at the crowning of your British kings.'

Holmes had been listening with closed eyes to our visitor's account, his legs stretched out in front of him. He opened his eyes.

'Have you informed the Bulgarian police?' he asked.

'My dear Mr. Holmes, to inform the Bulgarian police must, in the shortest of runs, inform the world. This is what I particularly desire to avoid.'

My companion motioned towards the chamois leather bag.

'You have told us why it is of such value to your country but as yet not the extreme urgency for its recovery.'

'I can only hint at the reason,' came the terse response.

'A hint will suffice for now.'

'It concerns my eldest son Boris.'

'Of what age?' Holmes probed.

'He is six.'

'Some more facts, please. Do we deduce there is some nationalistic or religious ceremony you wish your son to undergo which requires the presence of this manuscript?'

The Prince inclined his head.

'I repeat, Mr. Holmes, it is absolutely vital the Codex is found and returned to the nation. Otherwise—' His voice fell away.

'Your Royal Highness,' I intervened, 'if, as you say, you are acquainted with my chronicles you will know Sherlock Holmes—with the rare exception—is more intimately concerned with matters of murder, far removed from international politics.'

'You need only concern yourselves with the recovery of the manuscript, a simple theft,' came the reply. 'You may leave the politics to me.'

He rose to his feet and stood looking down at us. In a quite agitated manner, he said, 'Gentlemen, time is of the very essence. My country is surrounded by a plethora of warring nationalities and terrorist groups—Young Czechs, Italian Irridentisti, pan-Slavs, the *andartai* from Greece, the *chetnitsi* from Serbia. Worst of all, the Russian bear growls outside the cave, waiting to swallow me up. The fate of millions may depend on the swift recovery of this national treasure.'

My comrade asked, 'The Tsar of Russia, you suspect he is behind this theft?'

For a moment our visitor wore a bitter look.

'I see the Tsar behind everything,' he responded fiercely, 'as will you, I am sure. He wreaks his vengeance with the atrocity of the barbarian. The wretch has allocated a million francs for my assassination. Russian gold and Russian explosives are deployed against me everywhere. In his lair far away, barricaded by ice and eternal snow, guarded by four million soldiers who only ask to die for him, what has that monstrous sturgeon to fear?'

'You think, sir, that unless this manuscript is recovered there will be war?' I asked, even now unable to hide my incredulity.

'When I say the fate of millions, Dr. Watson,' the Prince replied, anger in his voice, 'I do not mean simply the fate of a few peasants and a Balkan Prince. I mean entire civilisations and whole empires.'

He went on, 'Thomas Cook's on Regent Street will make all your arrangements for a swift departure. Once you get to Paris, my private carriages on the Orient Express will be at your disposal.'

Our visitor started towards the door.

'Find your way to the Gare de Strasbourg by Friday evening, I beg of you,' he continued. 'Your tickets will be marked Sirkeci. That is the terminal by the Golden Horn. I request you switch to a Second Class carriage at Marchegg. There are eyes everywhere. Quit the train early, at Orşova on the Danube. Three hours after your arrival at Orşova a steamer, the *Orient*, of the Austrian Danube steamship company will dock. Board her. She will take you across the river to Svishtov. You will have arrived in my country. A highlight of your stay will be the International Sherlock Holmes Competition.'

The Prince Regnant reached the door. 'Mr. Holmes, if you are to use your powers, it is essential you are taken to the scene of this abominable crime the moment you arrive. Even considering the case of the Bruce-Partington Plans, you will never have had so great a chance of serving your country.'

'And the place where the Codex was concealed?' I asked, glancing across at a shelf of Baedekers.

Our visitor's eyes widened. He fell backwards in an exaggerated fashion, hands up. In a hushed tone he said, 'Dr. Watson, I must beg your indulgence. I know that landladies are sometimes curious as to their master's affairs. Can you guarantee that Mrs. Hudson is so rich she would refuse to divulge such information in the face of 500 grams of virgin Russian gold?'

At our silence he went on, 'Of course you cannot! May I merely say it is a day or two's journey from Sofia? I shall take you there myself. We shall slip away from my Palace unnoticed.'

Holmes had remained silent for some few minutes, his brows knitted and his eyes fixed upon the fire. At his quiet nod I stood up and went to our visitor, extending my hand. 'Your Royal Highness, you may leave everything to us. The very least we can guarantee is our best effort in the recovery of such a national treasure.'

I held the door open. 'One last question,' I continued. 'I have never heard of the International Sherlock Holmes Competition. How long has it been a tradition in your country?'

'This will be the first,' our visitor replied. 'I have just invented it. We Balkan Princes can do that sort of thing.'

Concerned, I enquired, 'But surely the whole point of our investigation will be our anonymity?'

'Dr. Watson, would you prefer to come to my country disguised as Sufist missionaries? Better my enemies can't see the wood from the trees. If there is a chance sighting of Mr. Holmes, they will not know if it really is the world's greatest deductive reasoner, the most energetic agent in Europe, or one of a hundred personators putting themselves forward for a considerable prize.'

He pointed to the outside world where dawn was about to break.

'Now, gentlemen, like the vampires which teem in my country, I must leave you lest your sunlight strikes me and *Ego mortuus sum.*'

With a further sweep of the blue cloak and a ring-bedizened hand, our visitor was gone, his exit as theatrical as his entry. Behind him lingered the faint aroma of Astrakhan lamb. We moved to our posts by the window to observe his departure down Baker Street in the spring dawn light. A single cab splashed its way past him from the Oxford Street end. A street-organ grinder loosened up for the morning rush with 'Soldiers of the Queen' and the swing-step of 'The British Grenadiers'.

Holmes turned away from the window with a wry expression. 'Well, Watson, what do you make of it all? Is my little practice degenerating into an agency for recovering ancient superstitious scribbles and giving advice to governesses?'

For a moment I feared he would back away. 'Holmes,' I replied quickly, 'I remind you that the affair of the blue carbuncle and *The Adventure of the Copper Beeches* first appeared to be a mere whim yet developed into serious investigations.'

* * *

Holmes is not a man to lose time in idle preparations. In his more intense moments he will permit himself no food. He once confided that his principal diet before we entered Mrs. Hudson's establishment was bread, potted meat and bacon cooked over a gas-ring. Before breakfast-time on the morning of our departure for Paris and the Gare de Strasbourg he took his hat and started off down the street.

With no intention of falling into this habit, I rang the bell for Mrs. Hudson and urged her to bring me one of her best breakfasts. I settled down to partake when my comrade's voice commanding our landlady to order a cab came up the stairway. He entered the chamber and glanced at my plate. 'Watson, you must abandon our virtuous landlady's excellent devilled kidneys and kedgeree. We have an assignation with brother Mycroft at No. 10 Downing Street. Pack a box as quickly as you can. We must depart within the half-hour if we are to continue onward to catch the boat-train to France.'

I sprang to my feet.

'Why does Mycroft wish to see us?' I asked, 'and why at No. 10? Why not the Diogenes Club or his home in Pall Mall?'

'Mycroft is a valued member of the Prime Minister's Kitchen Cabinet and the European Secretary's most valuable confidante. We are to take a small gift for our Balkan prince together with a confidential message conveying our Government's high regards. I ask you, Watson, are you at all averse to this trip? Would you like to give it a miss?'

'Not for worlds, Holmes!'

'Excellent!' came the reply.

I started towards my dressing-room. Unsure whether our investigation would stretch into the hot Balkan summer I continued on to the attic in search of tropical wear. I uncovered a set of clothing obtained from Gieves of Old Bond Street before I embarked for India—a now-elderly pig-sticking pith helmet with spine-pad, duck clothes and two palm beach suits. I returned the pith helmet to its tin topee case, the clothing to the Pukka wardrobe trunk, retaining a tropical suit in the form of tussore. When the original brownish colour of the strong coarse Indian silk turned to yellow it became the subject of considerable amusement at the Punjab Club, obliging me to stop wearing it. I decided it might look quite subdued in the Balkans among the Kurds, Druze, Jews, and Ismailis.

My comrade called up, 'Watson, along with your toothbrush and a half-pound box of honeydew tobacco, perhaps you would be good enough to bring those forceps you used in Kandahar to extract bullets from the living flesh. Mycroft worries that any shot intended for the Prince may well hit his travelling companions instead.'

CHAPTER III
ON HER MAJESTY'S SERVICE

I PULLED *Rupert of Hentzau* from my shelf of unread books. Given the lawlessness of eighteenth-century Scotland, when armed smugglers operated along the coast and thieves frequented the country roads, I decided to accompany it with a Walter Scott, *Guy Mannering*.

A goodbye to Mrs. Hudson and we were on our way. After a rainy night a fog had descended. The comfortable brougham edged us towards our destination via W.E. Hills of New Bond Street to drop off Holmes's fiddle for restringing. My comrade's careless scraping provided the proprietor with a regular client. From there we whirled around Trafalgar Square and down a cluttered Whitehall to Downing Street. A servant led us along a maze of corridors and up and down narrow uncarpeted stairways to a small chamber deep in the interior. Mycroft, portly as his brother was thin, rang for tea, welcoming us with the words, 'Gentlemen, the Prime Minister himself asked me to invite you here.'

'And why precisely has Salisbury taken this sudden interest in our humble lives?' Holmes asked.

Mycroft was solemn.

'He wishes me to tell you that Bulgaria looms high on his list of concerns. The disappearance of the Codex and your invitation to recover it are at the very least serendipitous. He begs you not to take this commission lightly.'

'Why has Bulgaria toppled the Back-Veldt Boers in your list of preoccupations?' I pursued.

'Europe is an armed camp, Bulgaria the powder-magazine. The Tsar of Russia yearns to wrest the throne of Bulgaria from the Catholic Prince and replace him with an Orthodox ruler.

The Tsar's armies lie gleaming and glittering at the Bulgarian border. If just two of Ferdinand's towns on the Danube declare for Russia, the Tsar will order his forces to attack.'

He waved us to our seats and went on, 'In response, this will trigger an immediate attack on Russia by the Austria-Hungarian Emperor. Then the French would mobilise. They have a secret reinsurance Treaty with Russia and would immediately join in on St. Petersburg's side. In turn, the Germans would come in against *them*. Meanwhile the Russians could wipe out the Turkish and Bulgarian Black Sea fleets in a single engagement. We would see the Tsar's warships steaming through the Dardanelles and the Bosphorus, threatening Her Britannic Majesty's routes to India. The balance of power we have striven to maintain since Bonaparte would be overthrown, the threat to our Empire significant.'

Mycroft pointed to a wall-map. 'The moment your boots touch the soil of Bulgaria you will be in topsy-turvy land. Balkan geography is complicated, the history intricate, the politics inexplicable. Certainty becomes uncertainty, the unexpected the prosaic. Nothing you take for granted in England will offer you a blueprint for your stay. Bulgaria is a land of danger, plague, treason and sudden death. You will feel you are forever on the edge of something unexpected. The Prince rules a Balkan state which has just awoken from a quincentennial sleep. The Capital Sofia is little more than a Turkish provincial town, some thousands of people crammed into ramshackle one-storeyed wooden houses, every saloon bar and lodgings infested like Agadir with the secret agents of the Great Powers. It is the odiferous monument to half a millennium of Ottoman civil maladministration, the squalor relieved solely by its fine setting on the slopes of Mount Vitosh.'

'Mycroft, what more do you know about our client?' I asked.

'Only that he is not to be taken lightly, addicted as he might be to table-rapping, palmistry, and crystal-gazing,' came the reply. 'The owner of a face dominated by a Bourbon nose and huge ears may have the look of the Maharaja of Mysore's legendary white elephant but his wily nature suggests the quality of the fox. The Foreign Office believes he may have something rather larger in mind for the Codex than the ceremony he mentioned.'

'Namely?' I pursued.

'The struggle of the Cross against the Crescent. He has aspirations to throw off the Ottoman yoke and resume the ancient Bulgarian title of Tsar.'

Mycroft stood up. 'But before I forget—' He took hold of a fine ebony-handled sword stick, withdrawing a thin triangular-section blade about three feet in length. The silver ferrule bore a lozenge-shaped hallmark indicating a French origin. He returned it to its cane sheath and passed it to Holmes.

'We would be grateful if you would present this to Prince Ferdinand. It was a personal gift to the Prime Minister from the President of France but the *Knyaz*—as he is addressed in Bulgaria—may be more in need of it in Sofia than the Marquess here in London.'

He looked hard at his brother. 'Sherlock, I ask you not to adopt your customary sneering approach to Royalty and the Aristocracy. This *opera buffa* principality may be in the hands of a minor Coburg but he surrounds himself in an icy hinterland of horror. Like Henry VIII he sleeps on eight mattresses rolled upon daily by his bed-makers to be sure assassins haven't stuffed them with poisoned daggers. He survives through absolutism tempered by assassination. In some parts of the Balkans suspected enemies are denounced and dragged off, convicted within the hour of treasonable conspiracy on the flimsiest evidence, and sentenced to indefinite imprisonment in the dungeons of a distant fortress. Rulers like Ferdinand have learnt the quieter ways to rid themselves of their enemies—a carriage accident with a runaway horse, a shot fired at night in a deserted street.'

He continued, 'It is rumoured Ferdinand dabbles in unusual '-ism's, such as occultism, cabalism, and spiritualism. Persons suspiciously like Black Magicians flit around and inside the Palace at various times. People swear that each day in the Palace grounds Ferdinand buries the gloves and ties he wore that day, intoning strange sentences with a mysterious air. In reality the menace to his world comes not from malign spirits but from a pocketful of far graver '-isms': militarism, imperialism, and nationalism.'

Mycroft walked around us to the door and turned to face us.

'I am instructing the British Legate in Sofia to meet you at the earliest possible opportunity. His name is Sir Penderel Moon. He will give you a complete briefing on the Prince. There is someone else I should mention—Colonel Kalchoff, the War Minister, a dangerous man. We intercept his telegrams. He leans strongly towards Berlin. If war threatens between England and Germany, he could convince Prince Ferdinand to take the Kaiser's side.'

His face took on a lighter expression. 'Gentlemen, I'm sorry your tea failed to arrive. No. 10 Downing Street is littered with the skeletons of *bonnes* who starved to death trying to find this cubby-hole. Dr. Watson, I hope you have packed your Norfolk jacket and knickerbockers, with a cloth cap for your head in the Balkan sun. The fishing is remarkably good, and wild-duck shooting is as excellent as in the fens, You might bag a capercailzie. The Prince is keen on blasting away. At the

Imperial shoot at Spala last October the *Times*' correspondent rated him the worst seat on a horse but the second-best grouse-bagger among the whole of European royalty. Only our own Prince of Wales is a better shot.'

He opened the door. 'I envy you both. A few days in the Prince's private carriages on the Orient Express, an hour or so aboard the ferry crossing the Danube—no enteric fever in the Balkans at present.'

A member of the Downing Street staff led us away. Mycroft called after us, 'Sherlock, I have a personal request. Ferdinand adores generals' uniforms, of which he has a great many. Do bring one back for your brother from your grateful client. It would go down wonderfully well at the Diogenes Club.'

CHAPTER IV
IN WHICH WE SET OFF FOR BULGARIA

WE quit Downing Street and boarded our train for Dover and beyond in good spirits. Holmes pulled on his striking Poshteen Long Coat with its many flaps and pockets and mesmeric promise of distant mountain ranges. The Capital's murk had deepened. Half-obscured Hawksmoor spires, the indissoluble chaos of grey wheel traffic confounded in nebulous London fogs, and a perpetual ring of tram-horse hoofs fell away behind us. Soon we lost sight of the Thames and the river's long reaches which I shall ever associate with our pursuit of the Andaman Islander in the earlier days of our career.

Half an hour or so down the line we halted to allow an oncoming train first use of a narrow tunnel. Below us, flowers on the sunny embankments slowed their rush the other way and allowed full examination. Comfrey with its bell-shaped, creamy yellow flowers stood guard over Common violets. Golden celandines with foliage as rich as liquorice grew side by side with figworts and patches of pink, blue and Tyrian purple milkwort.

I reflected on the bag of gold and banknotes tucked safely in our strong-box. Fees of this order underwrite Holmes's generosity. Despite the vexations of tax collectors he turns away commercial offers of a most tempting kind. Recently a German pipe manufacturer offered attractive royalties for permission to produce a Meerschaum in the shape of Holmes's head ('emphasising your fine aquiline nose'). Royal Tunbridge Wells offered a fine payment 'if you would let the Town Fathers raise a bronze statue to you next to one of Daniel Defoe', portraying Holmes drinking the Spa's ferrugious waters, over a brass plate affirming the springs 'are favoured by Mr. Sherlock Holmes for the maintenance and improvement of his deductive skills', and that the water would 'cure the colic, the melancholy, and the vapours; make the lean fat, the fat lean; kill flat worms in the belly, loosen the clammy humours of the body, dry the over-moist brain'. A small film studio offered to make him 'famous in every part of the world, from darkest Africa to the empty quarters of Mesopotamia', if he would also cover the cost of making 'Sherlock Holmes, the World's Paramount Consultant Detective'.

At Dover we caught the *SS Victoria*, a graceful steam-boat constructed to order by the Abdela & Mitchell yards on the Manchester Ship Canal ('Constructors of ships for the Nile, the Niger and Peruvian Amazon'). Our fellow passengers were mostly foreigners returning to Continental homes, and a scattering of English. The water was choppy in the aftermath of the storm. The heaving and yawing made me feel nauseous. I turned for distraction to the sheaf of papers pressed upon us as we quit Downing Street. In the margin Mycroft had scrawled: 'We watch events unfolding in the region with trepidation. Bulgaria is pivotal. On three sides empires are disintegrating like great suns which have reached their end. We hope for the best, that these old empires will die peacefully in their sleep, but fear the worst. Even though Bulgaria may occupy a mere paragraph in an English history hundreds of pages long, among those ageing empires she bulks very large. Nevertheless, England holds the scales. If required, and despite a hullabaloo from Little Englanders, the British Empire must show its teeth. If it must, it will bite.'

To my relief the ferry, delayed by the residue of the storm, at last reached the calm waters of the French port. We boarded the train to Paris. By evening we were at the Gare de Strasbourg where the Orient Express was on the point of departing. A porter hurried us from our landau to Prince Ferdinand's private carriages. Known in diplomatic circles as the Bulgarian foreign office on wheels, the compartments were an elegant marvel, the equal to the Pennsylvania Limited as the very quintessence of luxury, '*un vrai bijou d'intimité voyageuse*'. A brass plate indicated the London & North-west Railway company constructed the carriages, the same yards which provide carriages for our Queen-Empress's journeys to Balmoral. The door handles of the toilets bore the Prince's coat of arms. The furnishings had been purchased in Vienna as a job lot at a sale of a bankrupt lady singer, giving the whole a raffish Biedermeier femininity. Within minutes the *maître d'hôtel* handed us the evening's menu, a choice of oysters, soup with Italian pasta, turbot with green sauce, chicken à la chasseur, fillet of beef with château potatoes, chaud-froid of game animals, lettuce, chocolate pudding, buffet of desserts. In such unparalleled luxury, Holmes and I sat through the first evening in thoughtful mood and silent companionship.

It was rare to be on a case with my comrade-in-arms in foreign parts. Several of Holmes's greatest successes had been overseas without me or my service revolver at his side, among them the case of the Trepoff murder in Odessa, and his famous investigation of the sudden death of Cardinal Tosca (an inquiry carried out at the express desire of His Holiness the Pope). Neither had I been with him in Narbonne and Nimes in the well-paid service of the French Republic, nor during the singular tragedy of the Atkinson brothers at Trincomalee. There was, however, one never-to-be-forgotten journey when we travelled together to the Englischer Hof at Meiringen in search of ex-Professor Moriarty. Faithful readers will know of the shattering events which took place at the nearby Reichenbach Falls, events culminating in the death of the Napoleon of crime and the commencement of Holmes's Great Hiatus.

An uneasy feeling overtook me as I recollected Mycroft's words of warning: 'Remember, Bulgaria is the only place in the world where you can go out in the morning any day of the year and get blown up by a bomb intended for someone else.'

Spurred on by uneasy memories of Moriarty and thoughts of assassination, I caught my friend's eye.

'Holmes,' I began, breaking in to his reverie, 'I should like to extract a promise.'

My comrade sat up at attention, his pipe halfway to his lips.

'A promise, my dear chap?'

'That when I pass on to the Silent Land my earthly remains may be buried next to yours.'

Holmes eyed me inquisitively. 'A curious topic, Watson, my dear friend, though I perfectly accept it is stupidity rather than courage to refuse to recognise danger when it may be close upon us. Even the cat runs out of lives eventually.'

I went on, 'If by then you have purchased your bee-farm in the Sussex Downs—'

'I assume you wish to be suitably distant from the hives of Italian bees?'

'At least the quarter mile.'

'And if you predecease me do you promise on your own dear mother's grave not to rise up and haunt me?'

I held out my hand. 'A deal, Holmes.'

'Not yet, Watson. We have further negotiations to navigate before we shake on it. Can we agree a villager's chain between us? I am a light sleeper in life, I shall expect to be so in the sleep of death. To bear your snores has been a singular penance in my present incarnation. For eternity it would be quite intolerable.'

'At least the chain then,' I agreed promptly.

'And how would you like to be laid to your rest—in tropical sun-helmet, khaki uniform and puttees?'

'That will do nicely, Holmes, yes.'

'And what inscription on your stone?'

'I prefer to leave that to you, my dear fellow, but a reference to the Watson Codex and my medical duties in Afghanistan would not come amiss. I also remind you that you are my junior only by a year or two.'

'I think 'Steel True' would do.'

With unexpected sentimentality he added, 'When you go to your grave, all the high-collared young men from the West End will go to their offices with crape bands tied around their top-hats. They will hold your death a horrible thing.'

Thus in perfect jollity and good fellowship the placement of my grave if not the wording on my stone was settled.

CHAPTER V
WE CONTINUE OUR JOURNEY ON THE ORIENT EXPRESS

ON the morrow I rose early from a comfortable sleep, lulled by the sonorous puffing of the train at speed. Morning had broken bright and cloudless. Enchanted lands with their differing languages and scripts came and went, slipping behind us in quick succession as the express thundered on. I made my way to the Dining-car where I found Holmes studying a pile of papers.

He looked up at my entrance. 'Watson, I have been reading up on our client's genealogy. It seems the Prince claims blood with every legendary figure of Europe's past. Do order breakfast. I recommend the omelette stuffed with shallots and chives, or I am sure they will provide you with a passable copy of Mrs. Hudson's grilled kidneys and devilled chicken, even a plate of cold ham and galantine.'

'And what of his wife? He made no mention of her that I recall.'

'He was in a marriage of convenience, to Princess Marie Louise of Bourbon-Parma, the daughter of Roberto I of Parma and Princess Maria Pia, of the Bourbon Two Sicilies. She gave him four children, Boris, Kyril, Eudoxia and Nadezhda.'

'And?'

'She died soon after the birth of Nadezhda.'

'So he is at present a widower?'

'Heavens, how well you must have slept! In addition to being a widower, of which we may hear more, Ferdinand possesses remarkable gifts for the natural sciences. He is a renowned botanist and entomologist, and a host of other '-ists': linguist, alchemist, philatelist, and a very considerable amateur artist. In short, he will not deny himself his own opinions on every subject under the sun—politics, music, architecture, Darwinism, spiritualism perhaps, matters of the kitchen.'

A uniformed attendant brought us a set of newspapers. Among the considerable pile lay the *Journal de Genève*, the newspaper which, a day ahead of the Reuters despatch, had published the first report of the death of Holmes and ex-Professor Moriarty on that fateful day nine years earlier.

The *Adevarul de Cluj* was the only paper which came with an English translation. 'Holmes,' I said with a chuckle, 'listen to this: 'Some Strange Happenings In Eastern Bohemia'.'

The article began, 'A man's skeleton discovered during excavations for a deep well in the village of Mikulovice may indicate the presence of a vampire coven. Fearing the deceased might return from the grave, he was sent on his final journey weighed down with a huge stone on his chest and another one on his head. "Only the bodies of people believed to be vampires were given such treatment," reports a local priest.'

The story continued, 'The site may be the world's first burial place for the Undead, people who are believed to rise from the grave, walk once more on the Earth to prey on the living. All the skeletons showed tell-tale signs of anti-vampire rituals. Some were weighted down, others had a nail driven through their temple, or variously debilitated and their heads cut off and faced downward so they should not find their way back to the world of the living. These funerary rituals indicate the bodies were the remains of *revenants* in the eyes of the villagers.'

This was followed by the most chilling fact of all: 'Some of the whole bodies were buried facing down in the hope that when the time came for the vampire to rise it would dig with claws on its hands and feet ever-deeper downward into the earth.'

The article went on to report a very recent case in the Romanian village of Marotinul-de-Sus. When a woman fell ill for no apparent cause, the inhabitants smelt the presence of a *moroi* (vampire). Around midnight, several relatives of a recently-deceased man dug up his corpse, fearing he had become the vampire. They split open the ribcage, and removed his heart. This was burned, and the ashes given to the sick woman to drink in water to escape the vampire.

'Holmes, what do you think of such goings-on?' I asked with a further chuckle.

My companion failed to answer. Instead, he stared out at the landscape rushing by.

CHAPTER VI
THE MEETING AT THE IRON GATES

BY the second evening our train had entered mountainous territories. Hills, rocks and mountains piled one upon the other. The great fir forests stretched downwards to the very verges of cultivated fields in the lower valleys. We breathed the keen air and the balsamic odour of the pine trees. Green softened into sfumato. High peaks towered above us, etched by deep, fast-flowing rivers and avalanche-threatened passes that seemed uncrossable even as we wended our way through them. At one point ice-melt roared over a curving precipice into a vast cauldron, recalling the infamous Reichenbach Falls from whose black depths endless clouds of vapour rise. We looked out on the dainty green of the fresh spring spreading through the mountain meadows, and for contrast to the virgin white of the lingering winter above, the peaks now turning red with the light of a sun long dipped on us in our gorge below. The Continental spring had warmed the granite beneath the thin soil. Patches of colour were springing into being, like exotic quilts laid between moss-covered rocks - corn speedwell, rusty-red columbine, hart's tongue, wild primula, violets, Lady's Smock. A further profusion of white clover clothed the banks of glittering streams.

Another night went by. With a jolting of carriages we arrived at the river port of Orşova. The Orient Express leg of our journey was at an end.

Our boxes waited on board while the railway staff unloaded a live Cossack bear and several enormous panels of St. Petersburg. The station master approached us enquiring if we were '*Milords anglais*'. He handed over a message from Sir Penderel Moon. The British Legate was in the vicinity and wondered if we might find time to meet him within the hour. He would await us at nearby cataracts on the River Danube known as the Iron Gates. I went in search of a fly while Holmes ordered porters to transport our luggage to the harbour offices of the Austrian Danube steamship company.

Some thirty minutes later, the carriage deposited us at the fabled Iron Gates, as formidable a creation of Nature as the Reichenbach Falls. The waters rush through the narrow granite defile in sheets of glass-like transparency, the sound coming to us like a distant piano playing a repetitive but pleasant melody in the key of G. Spray rolled up like the smoke from a burning house. Incongruous in the forbidding setting, a small picnic party of men, elegant in Eton jackets, panama hats and pearl-grey gloves leapt across the spray-damp rocks like the wild goats of the Khyber Pass. Two or three of them carried telescopes. Their voices came to us on the slight breeze, unsettling cries of the profoundly deaf.

An isolated figure sat on a promontory staring down at the gleam of the boiling waters. He caught sight of us and clambered across the boulders towards us with the uncertain leaps of a male in middle age.

'Mr. Holmes and Dr. Watson, I presume,' he said with a pleasing smile.

'Your Excellency the British Legate, we presume?' I replied on our behalf.

He held out his hand. 'Yes. I apologise for interrupting your journey. I wanted to meet you before you travel on to Sofia. I understand you are undertaking a commission at the request of Prince Ferdinand.'

His voice dropped. 'In the hope of recovering a certain missing treasure, I believe?'

I inclined my head with considerable misgiving. It would not help our investigation if the detail was already seeping through the Diplomatic Corps.

The Legate threw me an enquiring glance. 'May I ask if you have brought your famous service pistol, Dr. Watson?'

'I have, Sir Penderel,' I responded, 'but, as you appear to have heard, we are here to recover the Codex Zographensis, not to engage in shoot-outs.'

'You might well assume that searching for an ancient manuscript is hardly a death-defying act, but you are entering the Balkans,' the Legate replied. 'The weaponry used by assassins in the Balkans may be highly valued among archaeologists and the British Museum but it can inflict savage wounds or death. Just over there,' he pointed across the river to the Bulgarian frontier, 'a deadly game is being played out. The Prince is at all times exposed to injury or death at the hands of a well-known Russian-backed assassin. You will be travelling at his side into the most remote plains and mountains of the whole of Europe.'

'The Prince did tell us that—' I began.

'And you took it as a little joke?' Sir Penderel enquired gravely. 'I beg you not to. The peril is a very real one. Assassinations are in fashion right across Europe—here a Russian Tsar, there a French President. Why not a Bulgarian *Knyaz*?'

The British Legate leaned closer. 'A year ago, while the Prince attended a funeral service for a Bulgarian general—who had himself been assassinated—an infernal machine concealed in the roof exploded. More recently, a Palace chef put typhus germs into the royal soup, which made Ferdinand extremely ill.

41

To greet the Prince's return to Sofia this month, the Chief of the Russian Secret Police sent him an infernal machine disguised as a box of the finest cigars. The Prince thanked him profusely and used the device to assassinate one of his own enemies.'

'And the remedy?' asked Holmes.

'The Prince must ensure the succession. He must remarry. Ferdinand needs a wife who will succour the Crown Prince and curry public favour through charitable endeavours. Above all, she must stand in for him at public occasions where his life might be most at risk.'

Sir Penderel smiled at a separate recollection. 'Prince Ferdinand once asked me whether I thought it feasible that he could gain the hand of one of our dear departed Queen's granddaughters. "Think of it," he said. "A grand-daughter of the Queen-Empress of England! Granddaughter of the Tsar-liberator! Cousin of the German Kaiser! A future Tsarina of All the Bulgars!".'

'And how did you respond?' I asked.

'In the finest traditions of the Foreign Office. I prevaricated. The cure would be worse than the ill. Whichever Royal House agreed to give him their daughter's hand would immediately encounter the overwhelming force of St. Petersburg's enmity.'

In the same serious tone he continued, 'The outside world considers Bulgaria a suitable subject for light operetta, a tiny State between the Danube and the Balkans, where the diplomatic activity of the Capitals of the Powers reaches its ruler muffled as by a deep blanket of snow. The reality is otherwise. The Russians present a most imminent and pressing danger. The Tsar aspires to place one of his Grand Dukes in the Palace of Sofia and make Bulgaria a Russian cats-paw where not a mouse would stir in the Balkans without his permission.'

He added, 'The Power most interested in checking Russian expansion is England. Mr. Holmes, if by the aid of the powers which you are said to possess you can find the Codex you will have deserved well of your country. As Her Majesty's Legate, I see a European Prince and future Bulgarian Tsar whose survival affords us the best chance of preventing a terrible calamity, a great war which could stretch from Moscow to the Pyrenees, from the North Sea to Palermo, a war in which tens of millions might die. I could not imagine a greater misfortune for the world than that this affair should end in your failure.'

In the distance a large ferry-boat chugged heavily towards us from the Bulgarian shore.

We turned and began to move towards the waiting coach. Sir Penderel brought us to a halt some yards short of our conveyance with the words, 'I would appreciate it if you will join me in a few days' time for a Royal Command performance of *Salomé* at the Royal Alhambra. I'm told it will be the first-ever performance in English. As it's Oscar Wilde, no doubt it will shock—but our louche Prince rarely misses the chance to be shocking.'

The diplomat reached out and shook our hands. 'A last word on Ferdinand. Like all opportunists he is inspired solely by regard for his personal interests. He pursues the *politique de bascule*. He coquettes with one Power, then another. You will find in him a great actor. He reinvents himself every time he jumps out of bed. He changes masks on the instant. He can be the polite, generous, debonair, sarcastic *homme du monde*, all smiles and amiability. That is his face to you. Or he can turn into a wily politician, his face to me. Or he may manifest himself as the near-tragic tyrant of a mysterious country, the easily offended ruler whose every susceptibility must be respected. That is his face to the Capitals of Europe.'

He added, 'There is one thing which unites all these princely faces—'

'Which is?' I asked.

'A complete lack of sincerity.'

We clambered into the carriage. Sir Penderel stepped back. 'Rooms have been reserved for you at the Hotel Panachoff,' he called out. 'When you set off in search of the Codex you will leave behind a Capital in fear. Each time the Prince journeys out of Sofia someone has their throat cut. Speculation is rife over which of the Prince's enemies will be murdered this time. A final request: when we are introduced at the Palace please act as though we were meeting for the first time.'

'You may rely on us,' I responded at once.

CHAPTER VII
IN WHICH WE ARRIVE AT THE ROYAL PALACE

THE *Orient* raised the Bulgarian tricolour of white, green and red and blasted its horn. We navigated the Iron Gates. The paddle-wheel churned in the milk-coffee waters and crossed to the steep right bank of the Danube, delayed a little by avoiding an immense raft of logs floating lazily downstream on its way to Black Sea, chaperoned by the inhabitants of ten or twelve huts on the roof. Ashore, a waiting Royal chauffeur handed us his card, 'Revitsky, coachman to H.R.H. Prince Ferdinand of Bulgaria'.

We embarked on the last leg of our journey. Cucumbers, tomatoes, cabbage, and peppers grew in neatly-tended vegetable plots. Storks nested on the roofs of monasteries, flapping their wings, their long, yellow beaks clacking as we drove past. A whiff of wood-smoke wafted in from the silent landscape, the most wonderful smell in all the world. In my somnolent state I dreamed of Delhi and the lean gun-horses streaking across mud hurdles at steeplechase exercise. I was transported back to the small villages of India when the twilight came and deepened into penumbra and a blue mist rose up from the fields, and, oddly, to the sweet-sour smell of the wraps of breast-feeding peasant women.

Several hours later Sofia hove into view. We came first to small manufactories of woollen cloths, linen and cotton stuffs, paper, soap, potash, copper and iron ware. Our tyres threw up a thousand smells. Nearer the centre the vehicle threaded its way through narrow streets, planks or logs laid on each side for foot-passengers.

We arrived at the Palace. The Bulgarian flag fluttered on a high mast alongside the Royal pennant. Except for the Taj Mahal it was the most beautiful building I had ever seen. The tall windows were framed by cretonne curtains which swung in the breeze. At dusk lights burned in every room to keep away the shadows, a hundred glass panes sparkling like the windows of the Palais Royal. Wide terraces fell away, with beds of scarlet geraniums lined with white oleanders and Judas-trees, dotted with naiads, dryads, nymphs and satyrs, and bronze deer from Herculanum. The side facing the terraces was surmounted by a pediment representing a boar hunt. Swallows by the hundreds swooped and soared out of nests along the cornices. Embroidered parterres spread out like tapestries, overlooking an immense lake which glinted like a sapphire, with richly caparisoned caïques circling to and fro across its black surface. All night the gardens and *orangerie* were illuminated by electric cars hidden in thickets.

At the sight of our vehicle, a company of the Prince's bodyguards commanded by a Major scrambled out from shaded spots to take up positions on every step of the broad stairway. They were resplendent in silver-braided scarlet uniforms with grey astrakhan caps and eagles' feathers held in jewelled clasps. Watching them stood a five-foot, long-legged grey sarus, almost motionless except for the slight quiver of its scarlet head and eighteen-inch-long, bayonet-like beak.

Our driver dropped us at the bottom of the Red Staircase, an exact copy of the gateway into the Kremlin's Palace of Facets where 400 years earlier Ivan the Terrible killed a messenger who brought him bad news. To one side, awaiting transportation to the kitchens, stood a pyramid of pomegranates, pineapples and Cassaba-melons.

We walked up the fifty-eight steps, receiving salutes. Above us, house-servants moved slowly back and forth across the entrance hall spraying essence of pine. A manservant invited us to dip our fingers in a holy-water stoop filled with violets. As I did so, I looked up at Holmes. With the Poshteen Long Coat open I could see his Accurate gold watch. As far as I knew, the watch and its Double Albert chain, together with a battered escritoire, two or three tie-pins and a snuffbox of old gold were the only heirlooms Holmes possessed. He caught my eye. A smile of amused anticipation flickered across his mouth. 'We must take particular care with our manners, Watson,' he murmured. 'There's not a spittoon in sight.'

We were guided to a large, refectory-like chamber, entering upon a scene so fantastic it could have been the residue of a tableau at Versailles. The floor jutted out over a terrace, giving the impression we floated in mid-air over a white sea. Every tone of red and blue mingled with gold. Cadets lined the walls, each dressed in a uniform of Albanian-Turkish appearance, with an embroidered scarlet tunic, and wide, multi-coloured silk cummerbund out of which stuck the handle of a *yataghan*, atop ample loose scarlet drawers.

The chamber was furnished with an organ and several pianos scattered around. A man sat at one of them playing a Haydn sonata which Holmes had taken to scratching out on the violin. The curtains and armchairs were covered with mauve or moss green velvet.

We caught sight of our client seated at an antique writing-table placed in the precise centre of the room. He was attired in a general's full dress uniform complete with white fur cap. His nose, a Bourbon inheritance, surged out and curved downward in a smooth arc. The pompous mustachios blossomed, the beard teased and trimmed in the way of the Valois Princes. The

Order of the Württemberg Crown, Grand Cross, was pinned to his tunic, above which could be seen the blazing red grand cordon of the Legion of Honour, once worn by his maternal ancestor Louis Philippe, the last king of France, and above that the Bulgarian Order of St. Alexander. Over him a giant chandelier hung from the stuccoed ceiling, a-drip with crystal stalactites, a gift from the House of Bourbon.

Watchful, to one side stood a man we recognised from Mycroft Holmes's description as the War Minister, Konstantin Kalchoff. He was almost engulfed by a group of military *attachés* wearing short beards of impeccable cut and blackness, the medley of uniforms glittering with decorations. Kalchoff was distinguished from his acolytes in being clean-shaven. His deep black eyes, a piercing look, the skin of his cheeks drawn quite tense over his outstanding bones, and the rather lengthened form of face indicated Tartar descent. The *attachés* spoke among themselves in low voices, every so often descending into whispers. Surrounding them like the defensive walls of Marrakesh were the attentive eyes and ears of the Prince's personal entourage—equerries, *aides-de-camp*, the officers of the Bodyguard. One or two wore *chapeaux de haute forme* and morning coats. Waiters carrying trays of heady *fée verte* wandered in and out of the circles like the rete of an astrolabe.

The Prince rose and came towards us. The faint scent of *violette de parme* had replaced the former smell of Astrakhan lamb. To my dismay he greeted us openly, as *étrangers de distinction*, as though to impress our importance on the onlookers. Without his curious disguise as the King of Bohemia, I was able to study him in more detail. The weight of fronting a predatory State was taking a corrosive toll. At around forty years of age, Ferdinand scarcely resembled the slim-waisted, golden-curled man who had accepted the throne of Bulgaria a mere decade or so ago. Only the high-pitched, drawling voice remained.

Sir Penderel stood nearby. The Prince drew us towards him. 'And this,' he said, 'is the British Legate—but he needs no introduction! You have already met!'

'I don't think so,' I began, remembering Sir Penderel's urgent request.

'Of course you have,' the Prince boomed. 'At the Iron Gates. Didn't you see my men with their telescopes, lip-readers all? Thank you for your kind words on that occasion, Sir Penderel: "a great actor" indeed!'

Momentarily we were left alone with Konstantin Kalchoff. He chose to address me first, his smile cold. 'Dr. Watson,' the War Minister began. 'As you are both a military and a medical man, are you on constant call to treat war fever at The Guards, or even Downing Street? Do the elderly gentlemen in your clubs speak of war with Germany and turn purple?'

'Why,' I exclaimed spontaneously, 'how on—?'

He gave a slight smile. 'I can assure you, your country is of the utmost importance to us even if to most Englishmen Bulgaria is a faraway country inhabited by a people about whom you know nothing and care even less.'

He paused, insistent on an answer.

'There is talk of a European war, yes,' I responded.

'Such nonsense,' came the instant reply. 'Modern artillery has made war improbable. Think of the damage a quick-firing one-pounder pom-pom can do, let alone the heavy Creusot with its ninety-six pound shell.'

'And the Kaiser? What is his opinion?' I interjected.

'As far as the Kaiser is concerned, a few concessions in Morocco and he could be kept quiet for a long time. He assured me himself that Germany has no other territorial ambitions.'

The Colonel gestured towards the Prince. 'What do you think of our Prince Regnant?'

I checked myself, and altered the turn of the sentence.

'Have you known each other for some time?' I countered.

'We met in Austria, on the artillery course at the Theresian Military Academy, long before his mother purchased the Bulgarian throne for him. I have been in his service and at his side ever since.'

'We understand the Prince is quite superstitious?' I offered.

Kalchoff broke into laughter. 'Look around you! Are there signs of the Kabbalah everywhere? Will he shoot every owl on sight? Does he believe a black cat passing on his left side is an omen so terrible he cannot speak of it without a shudder?' He added, 'Just as he sighs with pleasure if he encounters a chimney-sweep. Beneath that finery he wears a dozen, maybe a hundred amulets and lucky charms.'

Kalchoff dropped his voice. 'They appear to work. I know of two members of his household sworn to kill him if required. Daily at the Ministry for War we decode telegrams of the most compromising kind. This week we received information that a Russian explosives expert is somewhere among us, in Sofia itself, perhaps even in the Palace grounds, with a new kind of dynamite bomb invented in Paris.'

'Why does the Prince stay?' I asked incredulously. 'Why doesn't he pack up his treasures and return to Coburg to serve his ancestral land? Why not be a man of fashion amid the gaieties of Vienna and London and Paris?'

Kalchoff smiled. 'It's true he could drop anchor in a thousand water-holes if he chose.'

'Then?' I pursued.

'Shall I tell you his favourite saying?' Kalchoff responded. 'It is, "Better to reign in Hell than to serve in Heaven".'

The Prince was beckoning us over to a side-table. Turkish influence showed in tulip-shaped crystal glasses of tea and cut crystal cups filled with sherbet. Our client clapped Kalchoff on the shoulder and slipped an arm through his. Looking into the Minister's eyes, he exclaimed in a most amiable manner, 'Gentlemen, here you have my Minister of War, my dearest and most constant friend. He is an ally who preserves his balance in every emergency, a man of affairs who chose exile in Bulgaria over the delights of Vienna, the city where even the gods and goddesses of Olympus come in various disguises in search of Hebe. Konstantin stands guard over me in unremitting vigil like the Roman Centurion.'

The Prince turned to us. 'If you have recovered from your long journey, we shall leave in the morning. Our destination lies some days away. We shall travel incognito. There is a danger in travelling without several officers of the cuirassiers and a troop of cavalry but we must be as circumspect as possible. Fortunately, Dr. Watson, I believe we have your service revolver to protect us. You will be the sole barrier between me and the several enemies who seek my destruction. Without your protection, my life is not worth three days' purchase. As my Minister may have told you, there have already been five assassination attempts in my short reign, several of them by the Okhrana, the Russian Secret Service. Pyotr Rachkovsky is their chief. He takes to dynamite as saner men take to the opera.'

He stopped to stare around the room. 'Rachkovsky is becoming as familiar to me on the streets of my Capital as my own Chief of Police. I see him everywhere. In every corner. In every dark street.'

He ended our discussion with an ominous look and the words, 'One day I shall remove him from my path with the dynamite bought by his own roubles. His time will shortly come, gentlemen, as will the reign of terror of the Tsars themselves. I advise you to rid yourself of any Russian securities.'

Chapter VIII
IN WHICH WE JOURNEY TO THE CAVE CHURCHES

EARLY the next day we left the Hotel Panachoff and returned to the Palace. The Prince came down the Red Staircase to meet us. He carried a large pair of chamois-leather gauntlets. Goggles dangled from his neck. A white fur cap surmounted by a white plume a foot high sat imposingly on his head. A favourite flower of mine, a fresh Malmaison carnation, sprouted from his lapel. An immense handkerchief of very fine silk, coloured like parrots' tails, cascaded from a top pocket. His large, well-manicured hands were now even more luminous with costly rings. The absurdity of the plume combined with piquant knee-breeches and smart yellow boots made me warm towards him. My companion regarded him with a sardonic eye. "Slip out of the Palace unnoticed',' he commented, nodding at the ostrich feather.

Our salutations completed, Ferdinand led us to the stables, large buildings capable of holding a hundred horses. The great doors swung open. We entered upon another wonderland. It was like a harem of pure-blooded automobiles. Six of the latest and most elegant vehicles stood before us, the only motor-cars in the whole of Sofia. Each of the beautiful machines was assigned its own chauffeur. In some detail we were guided around the short and high five-litre Daimler, followed by the three-horsepower, curved-dash Oldsmobile which had fetched us from the Danube, and a Royal Mercedes powered by a Zeppelin airplane motor with an electrical gear shift. The Mercedes had been designed by the German Kaiser himself. Its rich mahogany doors were inlaid with floral designs of ivory and gold. The door-handle on the driver's side contained an ivory profile of the Prince Regnant. The handle on the other side depicted his deceased wife. Once a week, as though exercising three-year-old fillies, the chauffeurs drove the vehicles up and down the Stamboul Road, to and from the Prince's estate at Vranya, or a small distance further to his summer residence at Tchamkoria. Surrounded by nearly-impenetrable mountains, the road was one of only two or three routes in the whole of the country with a surface capable of supporting a motor vehicle.

Our host spoke nostalgically. 'As you see, even here in the backwater of Europe the motor-car enters our very stables. The fuel-tank replaces the corn-bin. In the last month alone I have laid off four coachmen, two grooms and seven stable-boys. In twenty years the Bulgar cavalry will be obsolete.' He shrugged. 'The pennants flying from their lances, steaming horses tossing their heads—the sabres glinting in the sun. Soon we shall see those splendid men crouching over the wheels of omnibuses, driving round and round grating gears.'

Unusually, the Prince had selected the least gaudy of his collection for our journey, a Lifu fourteen-seater wagonette. Steam-pressure was building up in the boiler positioned between driver and passenger. Butterfly nets and a set of killing jars jutted from the rear of the vehicle. A gardener was passing branches of an apple tree in blossom up to a servant on the roof-rack. Next came a large open trunk of provisions. The Prince's love of intricate dishes and succulent, highly-seasoned food was evident. We were to discover in the trunk, among other delights, salmis, mousselines, potted pork of Tours, and *bombes gaufrées à la pistache*, thrown together with a case of Calvados 1804.

'I am your chauffeur, my dearest guests,' the Prince announced grandly, pulling on the driving gauntlets. 'Our destination is the famous Red Church near the town of Perushtitsa.' His voice dropped. 'In fact, dear guests, I shall disclose our true destination once we are out of the city.'

At this he handed each of us a chic Panama hat for the journey.

With the Prince energetically at the controls we set off. The conveyance reflected in the window-glass of barbers, drapers and hosiers. Further on we slipped silently past larger establishments manufacturing cloth, coarse linen and canvass, propelled by the almost-silent steamer against the tide of peasants trudging in the opposite direction, some walking alongside wooden carts piled up with farm-produce for the market, drawn by long-horned oxen or black buffalo with bright greenish-blue eyes. A troop of cavalry resting in the shade of the old city walls jumped up with a rat-tat-tat of spurs to salute our driver, bayonets fixed, each man decked in a blue and silver uniform. Once through the walls our host turned half-back in his seat. 'Gentlemen, we go north east, our destination the monastery complex of Ivanovo, in the valley of the Roussenski Lom River.'

A few minutes more and we were in deep countryside of a disturbing and formidable kind, a strong contrast to the green and fertile landscape of Sussex where Holmes planned to locate his bee-farm.

To our right, high up on a dramatic cliff, surrounded by the silent loneliness of soaring mountains, stood the solid walls of a monastery which history recounts withstood the crashing waves of Turkish soldiery. An hour or so passed. Beneath us the paving gave way to furrowed dark earth. The hiss of the engine grew shriller. We passed isolated houses built of wood, two stories high, the lower part serving for a barn. Stands of pine replaced the wild pear, cherry, and crab-apple near sites of human habitation. A feeling of isolation grew more and more oppressive, alleviated now and then by horses spattered with glittering ornaments, blue beads, bells and amulets.

'You may shudder at the dismal wilderness around us,' the Prince called back, catching my thoughts, 'but it tells you Bulgarians are just like me. We would prefer to make our homes in barren mountains as free men, feeding on wild fruit and stale bread, rather than in fertile valleys crawling through life under the conqueror's yoke. Over there'—he pointed to a formidable mountain—'is the tomb of Vasil Lechkov, a Bulgar *borislav*, a great warrior. Lechkov went into battle with a cross in one hand, sword in the other. He hewed off fifteen heads before he fell against the Ottomans. According to the story, his men played nine-pins with them.'

Ferdinand added as an afterthought, 'though I understand Frenchmen's skulls make the best bowls—more rounded.'

Some miles later he spoke up again.

'Those mountains may provoke fear but they also provoke avarice. They are packed to the brim with topazes, amethysts, crystals, jasper.'

Another pause, then, 'You may have noted the absence of my wife. She died last year, twenty-four hours after giving birth to our fourth child.'

'The Princess must still have been very young,' I called forward sympathetically. 'Not so very young. Twenty-nine. I buried her in the Roman Catholic Cathedral of St Louis in Plovdiv.'

In his direct manner Holmes asked, 'Will you also be buried there when your time comes?'

'I plan to be buried in the Forty Martyrs Church in Turnovo, in a tomb as grand as that of my ancestor Louis XIV. Unfortunately the Coburgs don't have a Pope in their past or I'd book a plot on Vatican Hill.'

He went on, 'Like John of Rila, I shall take steps to embalm myself before death, consuming great quantities of Tansy and potions. People will make pilgrimages to my tomb, believing my incorruptible corpse will possess miraculous powers.'

With a rueful smile he added, 'First, however, before my death comes the matter of marriage. Sir Penderel and others will have told you the great vixen hunt is on. My darling mother, the Princess Clementina of Orléans, never forgets she is the daughter of Louis-Philippe, King of the French. You must meet her on her return with my children from Coburg. With quite indecent haste she is preparing everything for my next marriage. She has even designed a *fleur-de-lis* tiara for my bride, no doubt crowned with minarets and turrets and belfries. As to my diadem, she has consecrated it at Lourdes. It will rival that of the Russian Tsar in gems and beaten gold.'

He looked back over his shoulder. 'All that's wanting is that bride.'

'Why should someone so rich and powerful as you find it difficult to remarry?' I enquired. 'Surely it's simply a matter of time, a respectable period of mourning after your wife's death?'

The Prince chuckled grimly. 'Simply a matter of time, you say, Dr. Watson? I wish it were so. You may comprehend the lack of enthusiasm a woman of standing might have for such a marriage. Think of the fate of the Empress Elisabeth two years ago, stabbed to death in Geneva by an anarchist with a four-inch needle file.'

Night was coming on rapidly. It was almost dark before we saw a sprawling complex ahead. A big half-moon hung out of the heavens. The Lifu came to a stop at the Convent of Kazalak on the slopes of the Balkan mountains where we were to spend the night. Nuns brought us cups of coffee with small plates of rose-leaf jam and glasses of water. The younger nuns vacated their cells for us.

The Prince went on a long walk. He returned looking relaxed, carrying several specimens of rare flowers snatched in the gathering dusk for his botanical gardens in Sofia. The Mother Superior, an elderly brown-faced peasant woman, invited us to lay offerings before a miracle-working ikon of the Three Persons of the Trinity before leading the way across a cobbled courtyard to our beds. The Prince ordered us to meet for breakfast at six, ready to set off on the final leg of our journey.

I slept fitfully in my cell. Strange fancies and surmises and distorted countenances crowded into my mind. We were approaching territory as remote, bare and sinister as anything I had fought in during my long years in Afghanistan, when the blood ran fast. Memories of desperate encounters amid rifle-blazing crags flooded back.

CHAPTER IX
THE STONE WEDDING

WHEN morning broke, a scene of marvellous though savage beauty met our eye. On the eastern horizon, the caps of the great mountains lit up one after the other. We were soon on our way. The weather smiled and promised a fine journey. The Prince replaced cap and white plume with fresh headwear—a blue toque bordered with white astrakhan fur. We left the cloister in the bright early-morning light, passing old grey churches and convents. Valleys divided and sub-divided into many gorges, impossible to distinguish one from the other. Low-built whitewashed cottages sat in lonely rolling plains guarded by fierce, shaggy dogs.

Three hours went by. The silence inside the vehicle became oppressive. Holmes's characteristic disinclination to engage in small talk put the burden on me. I leaned forward experimentally.

'I understand we are in a region known for the frequency of earthquakes?'

I had struck a good subject.

'Certainly we are,' the Prince exclaimed. 'And I tell you, Dr. Watson, I adore earthquakes!'

'Well, sir, you are the first person I've met who adores earthquakes,' I replied. 'It must be an acquired taste.'

'I assure you, I adore them. The Earth gapes open, belching out scorching hot breath. Whole valleys like the one we are now in disappear. Once when I was over there'—he pointed towards the Eastern Rhodopes—'we had an earthquake every day for a week. You hear them coming. First a faraway whistling sound, then the thud of great boulders crumbling and sliding down with incredible speed, pushed by a gigantic hand. All living things, even the trees, trembled—except me.'

Another hour or so passed, mainly in silence. The sun grew warm and high in a brilliant blue sky. After the frugal breakfast on offer at the convent my thoughts turned to the extensive larder accompanying us on the roof.

'There!' the Prince exclaimed suddenly, pointing ahead. He brought the vehicle to a halt. 'Kamenna Svatba—the Stone Wedding. That is where we shall take lunch.'

The Prince re-engaged the clutch and we moved slowly forward, yawing on the badly-rutted track like the storm-driven cross-Channel ferry.

'Forty million years ago all this was at the bottom of a warm, shallow sea,' our host continued. 'Our famous volcanic activity created these rocks. Legend has it a young couple asked to be married here. According to folk-custom no one was permitted to see the bride's face. A strong wind came up and blew the veil aside and everyone saw her face. She was so beautiful even the groom's father desired her. As a punishment all the humans present were turned into those white stones.'

As he uttered 'white stones' the quiet was shattered by an immense explosion scarcely thirty paces ahead. Boulders and vegetation rose high into the sky. Shattered pieces of rock crashed down on the wagonette's roof. Angry voices yelled out from behind the rocky outcrop. The shouts were accompanied by a volley of reddish-yellow revolver flashes.

Shouting for Holmes to accompany me I fell out of the Lifu and crawled behind the sturdy vehicle, tugging at my revolver. Even before the debris ceased falling our host pulled out a silver-inlaid palm pistol. Displaying a reckless lack of concern for his own safety, he launched himself at the source of the shots, firing repeatedly.

The firing stopped. Two men jumped out from their hiding-place and sped away at a crouch, covering the boulder-ridden ground with remarkable speed. With a gesture of the deepest contempt, Ferdinand directed a torrent of words at them.

'Your Royal Highness,' I called out from behind the Lifu, standing up cautiously, 'that was as brave a—'

He cut me short with an airy wave.

'One gets used to these things.' He waved his empty pistol. *'Un des risques du métier.'*

He pointed at the lunch-boxes. 'Now the cowards have fled, we can get down to more serious business.'

'What was it they shouted at us?' I asked.

He replied, tersely, *'Tirani zai tooka ste luidi grabot ne Ferdinand!'*

I gave him a quizzical look.

'Macedonian. It means, "Tyrant! Know that here will be the grave of Ferdinand!".'

I asked, 'And your reply?'

'I shouted, "Assassin scum, lackeys of the spineless Tsar of Russia, run for your lives".'

'What made them flee from such a vantage point?' I asked. 'They could have picked us off one by one.'

'I also shouted, "I have here Mr. Sherlock Holmes and Dr. Watson. If you do not flee at once, with unerring aim Dr. Watson will let fly with his Adams .450 Mark III, the very pistol he used to such good effect in *The Hound of the Baskervilles*".'

Ferdinand stretched out his hand. 'By the way, do you recognise this?' he asked, showing the small pistol.

'A Philadelphia Baby Derringer,' I replied. 'Rather old-fashioned but still deadly close-to.'

'Not just any Derringer,' came the reply. 'The very one which John Wilkes Booth used in his assassination of President Abraham Lincoln on the night of April 14th, 1865.'

He clasped the pistol by the barrel and handed it to me. 'I shall be forever honoured if you might accept this as a small token of my high regard, as a souvenir of the danger we encountered here to-day.'

I looked round for my comrade-in-arms. Through all the commotion he had remained resolutely in his seat.

***

When he had chewed the last of the ortolans, the Prince sat back against the bride-and-groom pillar. It became clear he was in expansive mood.

'Mr. Holmes, Dr. Watson, I emphasise, a very great deal relies on your success in retrieving the Codex. Either the Balkans will set fire to the four corners of Europe or there will be tranquillity among our peoples,' he opined. 'If the latter—' He paused and threw us a most encouraging look, repeating, 'If the latter, I shall turn the Marquess of Salisbury's sword stick into a pruning-hook as commanded in Isaiah 2-4. There will be a great Peace banquet for the players—*oeufs à la turque, fillet de sole à la greque, faisan bulgare au blanc, pâtisserie Serbe, crème cardinal Monténégre*, and—' he gave a smile, 'finally a serving of Holmes-and-Watson Sponge with *crème anglaise de paix*. For that day I shall invite you to return to Sofia. Until then,' he added, with a further, more uneasy smile, 'pray for me.'

Chapter X
THE MYSTERIOUS RETURN OF THE CODEX

WE were now on the last leg of the journey to the setting of the crime. Through each tiny habitation, children ran alongside the steamer throwing capacious handfuls of sweet-smelling pink rose petals. If we stopped within the confines of a village—even for an instant—out popped the Mayor pressing small glass flagons of attar on us and rose-leaf jam to eat.

Once we left the Valley of Roses, the attar was replaced with bouquets of rare local flowers. In one village, our host was offered a cockerel which had grown a pair of horns. Eager for such curiosities, the Prince paid handsomely and had it loaded on the vehicle's roof.

The track now ran through the increasingly narrow valley cut by a river my Baedeker showed as the Rilska, made turbulent by numberless springs rising in the surrounding beech and pine. In the distance we made out a troop of wood-cutters beginning their business of cutting down the trees. The trees would be sorted into logs for the salt-mines or cut up for fuel, or to be converted into charcoal for the smelting and forging of iron. At the Reichenbach Falls, had Holmes died amongst those grim rocks rather than the fiendish criminal ex-Professor Moriarty alone, the world would have called upon the wood-cutters of Meiringen to bring him back for burial, let down by ropes to a great depth from the lofty overhanging and perpendicular rocks.

Ahead of us lay a landscape sodden with recent rain. Recklessly, the Prince ran the great vehicle onward, the front tyres throwing up ever-higher walls of muddy water, the steering wheel twisting wildly in his hands. Abruptly we slewed to one side and came to a dead stop. The Prince's efforts to drive us out of the mud by excessive use of the accelerator completed our misfortune. We were bogged down beyond the capacity of the Lifu to pull itself out. I stood by the wagonette's side looking anxiously ahead. The broken cliffs and beetling crags were worrisomely reminiscent of the time I was lost for a week with a half-section of infantry.

With the sun at its zenith I would normally have made use of the fine Panama presented by our host—certainly such fine headgear would complement my tropical suit—but I discovered on discreet enquiry that Panamas were among our client's favourite hats. I had placed mine under the seat, not wishing to mislead any sharp-shooter. We were well within shot of a Henri Martini.

The Prince gave up any attempt to drive out from the mire. He launched himself from the driver's seat and went over to a man in peasant garb quietly observing our misfortune from a short distance. Given orders and a gold coin by the Prince he hastened off. After some twenty minutes of awkward silence, a *fiacre* splashed towards us, drawn by long-tailed chestnuts two-abreast. The Prince gesticulated impatiently from the chestnuts to the depth of mud and water. Further orders were given. We engaged in another fifteen minutes of intermittent conversation before two white oxen hove into view; their forelocks dyed a bright orange to ward off evil. With a few heaves of their huge shoulders, the Lifu steamer was hauled on to drier land. We took our seats. The journey recommenced.

The limestone cliffs jutting up from tangled forest began to tower over us, every cranny and shoulder clearly visible through the telescope. If assassins lurked up there, we would be ground-bait. I was stirred as if I had been transported back half a lifetime to my Afghan days. As in other rocky deserts, there was no shadow of a sound in all that mighty wilderness; nothing but silence. Holmes too stared ahead, shading his eyes.

The vehicle could approach our destination no further. Our host stepped from the Lifu. He pulled down the three apple-tree branches from the roof-rack and handed one to each of us, holding on to the third. With this he waved us forward.

***

We entered a truly ancient world by a small, almost indiscernible opening in the rock-face. The Cave Monastery had been dug centuries earlier by Orthodox monks brooding over the mutilated records of the past. We went ever deeper into the cliff, through monastic cells, common rooms and chapels dedicated to the Archangel Michael. Murals stared out at us. One depicted in gruesome detail the suicide of Judas. On we went, through the St. Theodore Church and into the Gospodev Dol Chapel decorated with portraits of the saints Vlassius, Soridon and Modestus.

Finally the Prince pointed at a small stone marker sign set into the ground. 'There,' he said in an excited tone—'that points the way to the High Altar. Come, I shall show you. Relics have been stored there for safe-keeping since times gone by.'

At the stone altar the Prince placed his apple branch on the ground and leaned forward, pressing hard on an engraved consecration cross. Slowly the side opposite slid open.

'You see, gentlemen,' he began, beckoning us, 'this is where the manuscript—.'

The Prince's expression changed abruptly. He reeled back, staring wide-eyed at an open ornate circular box. Holmes and I leaned forward, following his gaze. Before us lay a bulky manuscript beautifully bound in buckram linen and silk.

'The Codex,' the Prince croaked. 'They have returned the Codex Zographensis! Mr. Holmes, despite all my efforts, word of your presence in my country must have leaked out and spread panic among the thieves.'

He stared down into the cavity in silence for some while, as though overcome. Presently he said, his voice deep with emotion, 'Thanks to you, the dark clouds which have surrounded my pathway are beginning to lift. This calls for the firing of a *feu de joie*.'

CHAPTER XI
IN WHICH HOLMES QUIZZES THE *KNYAZ*

CLUTCHING the ancient manuscript, the Prince led us back to the vehicle. We began the return journey to Sofia. To reassure the public and fend off ill-wishers and rumour, the Codex would be put on public display in a blue silk bag under heavy guard.

For almost an hour Holmes sat in silence at the back of the wagonette. It was clear when I glanced back he was revolving in his mind the bearings of this unexpected turn of events. At last Holmes broke the silence.

'Highness, there is only one point on which I should like a little more information. Why did you store the Codex in that cave church so far from Sofia?'

The Prince looked back over a shoulder and gave an uneasy smile. 'They say a dæmon spirit of the underworld called Rim-Papa expelled the monks from those caves and made their habitations his own. You saw how even I chose not enter the cliff without a branch from a sacred apple-tree bearing blossoms? The locals believe a subterranean world is entered through caverns, or hills, or mountains, inhabited by many races and orders of invisible beings, such as shades, fairies, and especially dæmons. The Three Birds live in such caves, birds which sing the dead back to life and the living into death. The whole country lives under a dense cloud of superstition. Even if thieves were told that I stored bars of the purest gold in the Altar stone few would dare venture a single step into the interior.'

'You concealed the Codex out here for that reason alone?' my comrade pursued.

'And because no lesser authority than your British Museum assured me such caves are ideal for the preservation of ancient parchments.'

'Namely?' Holmes enquired, leaning forward with interest.

'As you and Dr. Watson discovered, the air is absolutely clean and free of dust. The interior is in permanent twilight. And, being so deep in the cliff, it remains cool no matter the season,' the Prince finished.

'What temperature would that be?' I asked.

'A permanent 11° to 12° Centigrade.'

Holmes asked, 'How long has the Codex been stored there?'

'From the very moment I ascended the throne.'

'Which is—please remind me—how long?'

'Twelve years.'

'I see,' Holmes murmured with an enigmatic look.

No one spoke for a further two hours until our host indicated we were about to stop for a short respite. He brought the wagonette to a halt beside a cold, clear brooklet which sang like a swallow as it rippled by. The Prince stepped from the Lifu and gave a signal. A stream of servants emerged from the bushes and ran towards us. Two erected a green-lined parasol. Others opened cases and piece by piece brought out a richly-ornamented wine cooler, three Regency silver-gilt dinner plates and silver-gilt serving tongs. A further servant waiting his turn now appeared, carrying silver tureens which he placed one by one before us.

'For you, Mr. Holmes,' said our host, 'slices of roast beef, to be followed by treacle sponge with Madagascan vanilla custard. For you, Dr. Watson, smoked Scottish salmon—the very dishes which I believe you ordered at Simpson's Grand Cigar Divan.'

He sighed nostalgically.

'In my mind's eye I see Simpson's now,' he continued. 'The crystal chandeliers, the French-polished panelled walls, the roasts carved from the trolley.'

He pointed towards the volcanic rim of Mount Vitosh looming above us, its snow-tipped heights changing to rose and orange with the slow decline of the sun.

'But when I am there I must be here. When I am here I must be there. I am at peace nowhere for long.'

Chapter XII
IN WHICH HOLMES QUIZZES ME

THE Prince dropped us off at the Panachoff hotel. He requested, 'Dr. Watson, when you publish this adventure, I know you must give your comrade the best lines but spare a few for me. I hope I have not been unamusing.' At this he drove off, the cockerel that had grown a pair of horns still protesting on the roof-rack.

The Panachoff was a dilapidated yellow four-story edifice sited in pleasant gardens at the end of a long tree-lined avenue. In the heat of the day, the rooms were kept cool by tightly-closed wooden shutters. The occasional earthquake had caused heavy cracking in what was visible of the foundations. Although it was considered the best of Sofia's few hotels, the wood had not been fully seasoned before the hotel was built. As a result unpleasant insects abounded, disturbing our sleep.

We decided to remain in Sofia only a day or two more, long enough for Holmes to take part in the first international Sherlock Holmes competition and for us to be guests of the British Legate for the Royal Command performance at the Alhambra Theatre. Despite the unexpected return of the Codex, the Prince insisted we retain the handsome fee. In addition our generous client presented me with the Sanderson Mahogany Bellows camera which accompanied us to the caves but which remained in its dust-proof container on the Lifu steamer's roof. I determined to put the Sanderson to use during our return journey, diverting to capture for posterity the Alpine setting of Holmes's great triumph over evil, the Reichenbach Falls, the place of death of ex-Professor James Moriarty.

I dressed for dinner, emerging to find Holmes looking out on to the street. His face was rigid. An English language newspaper lay open on the table. He pointed at it.

'Watson, this was left for us by Sir Penderel. He has marked a piece on page two.'

I turned to the bold headline: ANOTHER ATTEMPT ON THE LIFE OF THE *KNYAZ*. FIERCE FIGHT.

I read aloud, 'Two days ago, while showing our beautiful land to eminent foreign guests, there was an outrageous and violent attempt on the life of His Royal Highness, starting with a great explosion followed by a volley of dynamite cartridges. Unfortunately for the assassins and their evil pay-masters, the Prince was not in the least intimidated. According to the eyewitness account of the Royal chauffeur, His Royal Highness leapt from the vehicle and ran straight towards the assailants. Made fearful by our beloved ruler's resolution, the assassins emerged like a plague of vermin from behind a boulder and rushed off towards scrubland. With shouts of scorn, the *Knyaz* fired several pistol shots, killing two attackers and wounding at least two more.'

A grotesque *nature morte* photograph accompanied the article. Two bodies were propped up against a stunted willow tree. The yellowy-white faces stood out in harsh and discordant contrast to the full Russian military uniforms in which they were dressed. It was known the Palace kept a supply of cadavers of failed assassins in reserve in a deep-freeze in the royal ice-house to put before the camera, clad according to the enemy of the day. One of the cadavers was the Russian agent Captain Nelidoff, executed some months earlier for his intrigues. Nelidoff's corpse in a variety of uniforms had been of particular utility. It had the further benefit of pricking the authorities in Peterhof.

Perplexed, I put the newspaper down. 'Holmes, we had no chauffeur except the Prince. I saw no evidence of shots from his palm pistol hitting our attackers. As to this photograph—'

Holmes stared thoughtfully out of the window, so engrossed in his thoughts that he hardly made a return to my observation.

'Clearly it was composed before we left Sofia,' he responded at last, with an abstracted look. He left his seat to take a few turns up and down, pacing the room with his head sunk upon his chest and his hands clasped behind him. Finally he turned to engage me.

'Watson, think back a little. When we set off on our journey with the Prince, how did he describe our destination?'

'You mean the monastery complex of Ivanovo, in the valley of the Roussenski Lom River?'

'Indeed, that was the location, but what of the direction?'

'North-east, he said.'

'Yet despite a principal thoroughfare heading in that direction we set off due east, towards the Eastern Rhodopes. Why?'

'To throw off assassins in our wake?' I offered. 'Even then, look what happened at the Stone Wedding.'

My comrade continued to look thoughtful.

'Perhaps,' he responded. After a while he continued, 'How would you describe our trip to the caves?'

'Distinctly memorable, Holmes.'

'Memorable, yes. And—?'

'The Prince was most companionable.'

'Yes, very companionable. What else, my dear Boswell?'

'Educational! I have never learnt so much about volcanic activity—phreatic eruptions, volcanic bombs, lapilli fragments! As to butterflies—!'

'Indeed, butterflies,' Holmes agreed, with an expressive tightening of the jaw. 'It will take weeks to clear out *Callophrys rubi* and *Erebia aethiops* from my brain's attic.'

'As to the butterfly the Prince himself discovered in 1886— *Cupido decoloratus*—'

'*Cupido decoloratus*, that too,' Holmes responded, his lips beginning to twitch. 'And the accounts of his botanical expeditions in search of the golden-yellow *anagallis*?'

'Holmes, beetles! His devotion to zoology. Do you recall him telling us of all branches of zoology, the study of insects is the most attractive to him, and of all insects beetles are the species with which he is most familiar? And what of his hero Hristo Botev? Botev's poem 'To My Mother', which the Prince recited with such feeling—?'

'Or his postage-stamps!' Holmes added—cruelly, given the undeniable fact I had completely missed the point of his interrogation. He continued, 'Are we ever likely to forget the several hours over our picnic meals looking through his stamp-collection?'

'As you say!' I enthused. 'What a wonderful collection. The 1845 Basel Dove, not to forget the 1848 Perot Provisional! What concern for our enjoyment of the journey. You must admit his hospitality is of the highest rank.'

'The highest, Watson. You are quite right to stress that. Therefore you will be providing your readers with an exact record of the hours His Highness regaled us with the circumstances of his birth—?'

'I shall consider it, Holmes,' I responded, rather taken aback, given my companion's well-known disdain for such things.

'—which, in case you did not take written notes at the time, went "I was born in Vienna, a Prince of the Koháry branch of the ducal family of Saxe-Coburg-Gotha, the Koháry being descended from an immensely wealthy Upper Hungarian noble family which once held the Princely lands of Čabraď and Sitno in Slovakia, among others".'

'Bravo, Holmes! I shall keep your pointers and suggestions to the forefront of my mind as I write up these events, never fear.'

'—that "At my birth on February 26, 1861",' Holmes went on remorselessly, '"I was given the title Ferdinand Maximilian Karl Leopold Maria of Saxe-Coburg and Gotha-Koháry"—'

'I believe I may have missed that detail, Holmes,' I replied, reaching for my note-book.

At this, my companion broke out into high-keyed laughter. 'Watson, enough! When I asked how you would describe our journey to the caves, I did not refer to the subjects of our—or rather his—conversations!'

'What then?' I asked, perplexed.

'I meant, by which means was our journey conducted?'

'For the most part in a Lifu steamer.'

'A vehicle capable of thirty-five miles an hour, is it not?'

'Even more.'

'So, I ask you, which phrase will you use to describe the manner of our journey to the caves? Will you call it break-neck?'

'No, Holmes,' I replied. 'I would not say it was break-neck.'

'Vertiginous?'

'Not vertiginous,' I replied firmly, my forehead wrinkling.

'Headlong, perhaps?'

'No, certainly not headlong.'

'Nor hot-foot, I suppose?'

I frowned again. Where was Holmes going with this?

'Not hot-foot, Holmes, not at all. I would not describe the pace as in any way precipitous.'

'Rather, shall we say, in due course, you will be describing it in your chronicle as leisurely?'

'I might do so, yes,' I replied, nettled. 'Thank you for that suggestion.'

'For example, while we refilled our vehicle's water-tank at Lake Srebarna, you will recall his lecture on the thirty-nine mammal species, the reptiles, amphibians and fish inhabiting the region, not to overlook the Dalmatian Pelican, the Greylag Goose, the Golden Eagle, the Egyptian Vulture, the Long-Legged Buzzard and the Ruddy Shelduck?'

'I do certainly recall such a lecture, Holmes, though not in the precise detail.'

'And our happy hours sitting in that peasant cottage among hens and two pigs while he discoursed in Bulgarian on his origins? Have you already forgotten?'

'I recall the hens and pigs perfectly, Holmes,' I replied with fast-diminishing patience.

'Where we were also informed in a series of illuminating asides that his father Augustus was a brother of Ferdinand II of Portugal and a first cousin to both Queen Victoria and her husband Albert, Prince Consort?'

'Holmes!' I cried out, by now too exasperated to offer a temperate reply. 'All right, I give in. Yes, the Prince did conduct us on a journey to the caves in a manner which could be termed unhurried, even-paced, even leisurely. We are guests in his country! For the love of heaven, may I ask what is your point?'

My companion's tone turned from teasing to grave. 'The point, Watson, is this: when the Prince arrived at our Baker Street lodgings—at the quarter to five in the morning, you may recall—he informed us he had hardly had a wink of sleep since the Codex disappeared, is that not so?'

'He did.'

'That the fate of his country and untold millions of lives depended on its speedy recovery?'

'That was what he told us, yes.'

'Furthermore, that the Tsar in Petersburg had long been plotting an attack, an invasion which could be prompted if news leaked out the Codex was missing, a massive military onslaught on this country from across the Danube which only the quick recovery of the Codex could forestall?'

'He did describe those possible consequences, yes.'

'And that its loss threatened a pivotal ceremony concerning his son?'

'Yes, Holmes. He laid great emphasis on that.'

'You took his concerns to be a fiction?'

'Not at all!' I cried. 'Both your brother Mycroft and Sir Penderel have led us to believe the possibilities of his overthrow are entirely real.'

'If the danger to his throne and dynasty were as immediate and grave as he portrayed it, we should have made a bee-line for the caves. Why did we not? Why so many diversions? The Prince's overriding aim should not have been to educate his guests in the flora and fauna of Bulgaria, nor the long history of its monasteries, nor the Penny Black or the 1855 Three Skilling Banco with the yellow colour error, nor the Coburg lineage according to the Gospel of Luke, not even the Long-Legged Buzzard and the Ruddy Shelduck—but to ensure THE VERY SURVIVAL OF HIS THRONE AND DYNASTY. The Stone Wedding was at least 40 degrees off the line we should have taken. Lake Srebarna meant a further diversion of half a day. Why such a leisurely and discursive ramble on the way to the scene of the crime? Can you explain that?'

Holmes looked away. It was clear he was to be left to his thoughts. I still held the newspaper in my hand. I was about to toss it down when a small entry deep inside caught my eye, mentioning my companion by name. It was a piece copied from the *Chicago Sun* reporting on the death of Elmer M. Anderson, the most famous of the Pinkerton detectives, the apprehender of countless criminals during his twenty-three years with the Agency. The obituary related his final hour. 'An intriguing account in the *Strand Magazine* of a murder solved, titled *The Reigate Puzzle*, was being read aloud to the dying man. Mr. Anderson lay in complete silence, apparently comatose, until the point came in the chronicle when the world-famous English Consulting Detective Sherlock Holmes revealed his deduction. At this, the dying man reared up in his bed. "That's got him!" he roared with delight. "By God, Holmes has done it again!".'

The obituary ended, 'Those were Anderson's final words on Earth. He departed life happy. A most admired fellow Consulting Detective had got his man.'

Chapter XIII
THE GREAT SHERLOCK HOLMES COMPETITION

IT was time to go to the Palace for the first International Sherlock Holmes competition. A carriage took us along city streets. Arriving at the Palace we were led through bustling corridors. The swishing of silk and buzz of voices grew louder as we approached our destination. A footman pulled open the large doors. What a sight met our eyes! The room was filled to every corner with the coloured whirl of uniforms. Folding Pocket Kodak cameras lay on almost every table. We saw military officers and officers of the household in full uniform, ladies parading in the latest fashions expertly copied from the great Parisian Houses along the Rue de la Paix, resplendent with blazing cabochon opals and otter cloaks and monkey fur boleros. Reds, greens, royal blues, violets. Not a tint was left on the colourist's palette. Gorgeously-clad attendants swirled around tables, waiting on Bulgaria's aristocracy. As the sun dominates the astronomical objects bound by gravitation in orbit around it, Ferdinand stood out, resplendent and absurd in a Bulgarian general's uniform and golden spurs. An outer ring of planets bustled with *attachés*, equerries and chancellors of orders and decorations. Elegant ladies in satins and taffetas, trimmed with tulle and lace, circled among marshals, grand almoners, chamberlains, and commandants of the Palace. Rustling skirts over high, wrinkled morocco boots swept the waxed parquet. By red-curtained windows stood more women guests, in colourful clusters of furs and ostrich feathers—each wearing a yellow beryl of the kind sourced only from the Ural Mountains, in

78

homage to Holmes's great success in *The Adventure of the Beryl Coronet*.

We were led to Sir Penderel's table. He stood up to greet us. Jocularly I enquired, 'In our brief absence how many bloated corpses of the Prince's enemies have been discovered floating down the River Iskar with their throats slashed?' to which the Legate replied 'Unusually, not one!'

A warm-up act much in vogue was reaching its climax on the small stage. Iannes the Occultist stood beside a young woman seated under a sheet. The woman conversed with the audience until the very second the magician whisked away the sheet. She had vanished without a trace.

My comrade-in-arms left us to join the four Bulgarian finalists. The Prince Regnant was fully up to date with our cases. The winning Holmes would receive an exact copy of the plaster busts of Bonaparte in *The Six Napoleons*, placed in a prime position on the podium. Several of the Bulgarian contestants wore deer-stalkers and puffed dramatically on Meerschaums. The real Holmes had opted for his ear-flapped travelling cap, a loaded hunting crop (his favourite weapon) and the briar-root pipe, the one he preferred before breakfast, composed of all the plugs and dottles left from his smokes of the day before, carefully dried and collected.

The Sherlock Holmes from Burgas sported a single eyeglass. The contestant from the ancient Capital Turnovo wore a facsimile of Holmes's award from the Nayeb-Saltaneh of Persia: the green ribbon of the Order of the Lion and the Sun. The entry representing the Capital was of the same height as Holmes at just over six feet. In one respect his attire exactly matched that of our client on his arrival at Baker Street that morning—a cyan cloak thrown over the shoulders, secured at the neck with a brooch. A fine pair of silken black mustachios emphasised the glittering black of his eyes.

The five-piece Gypsy band struck up the Bulgarian national anthem followed by a rousing version of the first six bars of *God Save The Queen* in honour of the land of Holmes's birth. The Prince made a short, elegant speech, referring to his deceased wife and how the money raised from the evening's donations would go to the charitable school she had founded for the Blind.

The band tuned up for a polka in two-four step. In time to the beat, the five Sherlock Holmeses trotted up the short flight of stairs to the platform. They arranged themselves in order, each holding a placard with a number from 1 to 5 in Roman numerals. The monocled No. III stood on one side of the real Holmes, the lavishly mustachioed No. V on the other, puffing hard at a remarkable skull-and-eagle meerschaum pipe. Each was obliged to address the audience in English, the language of the genuine Sherlock Holmes.

No. I was a small man representing Plovdiv. He wore a voluminous trench coat and carried a very large 10-power, silver and chrome magnifying-glass. He leapt from the platform and scurried around the nearest tables peering closely at the diners, grunting a succession of By Joves! and Humphs! and Tut-tuts! and Halloas!, his left eye grotesquely magnified into something both comical and sinister. He received hearty applause from the audience, but only a sprinkling of votes.

Next came the turn of the Sherlock Holmes from Sozopol boasting the green ribbon of the Order of the Lion and the Sun. In the fashion of the American actor William Gillette playing Holmes for the stage, he wore a long grey cape. From behind a curtain he brought out a penny-farthing velocipede with moustache handlebars and rode it unsteadily among the tables. He too received warm applause, and a small sympathy vote.

No. III was a Ribston-pippin of a man, no more than five feet in height. He took the monocle from his eye and waved it like a professor, proclaiming in a witty drawl, 'My name is Sherlock Holmes. As you can deduce, these others are counterfeits and should be arrested by our indefatigable Sofia police'.

Sir Penderel and I jumped to our feet applauding. Despite this show of enthusiasm ours were the only two votes he received.

No. IV, the real Holmes stepped forward. He swished the hunting crop in a deadly manner exactly as I had seen him knock a pistol from John Clay's hand in *The Red-Headed League* and drive away the adder in *The Adventure of the Speckled Band*. This was followed by a gripping account of his deductive methods from *The Hound of the Baskervilles*, how he had sniffed like a bloodhound at a curious remark in the butler's statement, that for the first part of his employer's night-time stroll, the footmarks were those of a man proceeding at a leisurely pace, but from the moment Sir Charles Baskerville left a gate, the observant butler Barrymore said his master seemed to be 'walking upon his toes'. Only Holmes had interpreted the phrase 'walking upon his toes' correctly—"the man was running, running desperately, running for his life, running until he burst his heart and fell dead upon his face".

It was a *tour de force*. Despite this excellent account, and despite the ubiquity of Mr. Sidney Paget's illustrations in the *Strand* portraying my comrade's considerable but not outlandish height and prominent, square-set chin, the real Sherlock Holmes was the only Holmes to receive no votes at all.

No. V from Sofia was met with a thunderous round of applause. Rather than a deer-stalker he wore a Girardi at a rakish angle. In excellent English, he at once took his cue from the real Holmes, picking up on another famed example of Holmes's abductive reasoning, in *The Adventure of Silver Blaze*. He related how he and I had travelled to Dartmoor, to King's Pyland, at the express invitation of a baffled Inspector Gregory of Scotland Yard. A valuable racehorse had been stolen on the eve of a famous race. Although a dog was kept in the stables, someone had been in and had fetched out a horse without the dog barking enough to arouse two stable-lads in the loft.

Word-perfect he quoted:

'Inspector Gregory: "Is there any other point to which you would wish to draw my attention?"

Holmes: "To the curious incident of the dog in the night-time."

Inspector Gregory: "The dog did nothing in the night-time."

By now almost the entire room was quoting my chronicle along with Holmes No. V. As one they called out, "That was the curious incident."

A clear winner, No. V stepped forward and gave a deep bow. For the first time in his pre-eminent career the real Holmes had been topped on his own territory, and by an impersonator. The Prince called out to the victor, 'Please reveal yourself and accept your prize!'

No. V swept the Girardi from his head and tossed it to the cheering audience. To even louder cheers and laughter he reached up to the glistening mustachios and peeled them off inch by inch to reveal the grinning face of the War Minister Konstantin Kalchoff. With a dart of a hand he snatched the hunting crop from my comrade, the real Sherlock Holmes. To the consternation of guests unacquainted with *The Six Napoleons*, he brought it down like a *canne de combat* on the head of the plaster bust of Napoleon, smashing it to pieces. Reaching into the debris he plucked out a small black gem and held it up. There was a general gasp.

'My heavens,' I whispered to Sir Penderel. 'Unless I am very much mistaken, that is the most famous pearl now existing in the world, the Tahitian pearl once owned by Rodrigo Borgia. It is reputed to bring death to its owner.'

The Sherlock Holmes Dinner commenced. The Gypsy band went into full swing with *'The Roast Beef of Old England'*. Within minutes waiters circulated, clothed and gloved in white. Little Dourga, the Hindoo dancer, had replaced Iannes the Occultist on the stage.

We were into the *Shkembe Chorba*—tripe soup seasoned with garlic, vinegar, and hot red pepper—when a messenger came to our table and whispered to Sir Penderel. In turn, the British Legate leaned across to us. He said in a low voice, 'Mr. Holmes, your assistance may be required. A Captain Barrington, an Englishman resident here, has gone missing. He is married to a very beautiful Bulgarian. He left their villa on horseback yesterday on a mysterious mission, saying he would be back by sun-up today but he has failed to return. In case something untoward has happened, would you and Dr. Watson pay Mrs. Barrington a call? I consider them particular friends.'

Holmes nodded his assent. He asked, 'Would you be good enough to describe Captain Barrington?'

'He has lived in quiet here in Bulgaria for about two years. In stature rather below his regiment's average, slim, with a waist that one might almost call pinched. In one respect he is similar to the Prince, his wonderful mustachios. They are as luxuriant as Ferdinand's own. He's as skilled as a Parthian in the saddle. I find it difficult to believe he would have fallen from his horse.'

Chapter XIV
THE STRANGE DISAPPEARANCE OF CAPTAIN BARRINGTON

THE next morning a phæton with extravagantly large wheels came from the British Legation to fetch us. Captain Barrington had not returned. We were dropped off at a fine villa near the Episcopal Palace. A maid took our cards into the interior. She reappeared and led us to a charming sitting room furnished in the English style.

Mrs. Barrington rose at our entrance. A light smell of English lavender came to us as we approached. She was slight, with small feet and hands. As linguistically gifted as the Prince Regnant, she spoke excellent and melodious English. She looked keenly at us, her aquamarine eyes—an unusual colour for a Bulgar—large and transparently clear, beneath thick, dark lashes. She wore a plain, tailor-made skirt with a white muslin blouse, the high neck supported by whalebone. Her hair was up in the latest fashion, coiled over the top of her head, puffed out into a great pompadour.

We were invited to occupy a sofa while our hostess sat across from us on a *fauteuil*.

The same maid who greeted us on our arrival returned with a tray of crystal glasses. Each glass of water held a long-handled spoon. Our hostess said, 'You must try a speciality of the region. Mastic. It is derived from the resinous part of a plant found mostly on the Ægean island of Chios. We say it brings sweetness to the conversation.'

On instruction we dipped the spoons into the white paste, washing it down with the water. I pointed at a cabinet photograph she held on her lap. 'Is that to help our investigation, Madam?'

She nodded. 'It is the photograph taken on the day of our wedding.'

She lifted it by the mahogany frame and held it forward to Holmes, adding, 'Please keep it with you for your search.'

My companion studied the photograph and passed it to me. It had been coloured in by an artistic hand. The smiling bride was magnificently attired in a Russian Boyar dress of gold-embroidered, mauve-coloured satin with a long overmantle of gold brocade and hanging sleeves of mauve velvet. On the plaited hair perched a large golden sun-shaped *kokoshnik* studded with pearls. She gazed out of the photograph with her head tilted in coquettish Dolly Varden fashion. In the background loomed the romantic and mediaeval image of Bodiam Castle in Sussex. The groom's dark mustachios *à la* Prince Regnant were as Sir Penderel had described, particularly impressive.

I returned the photograph to my companion. As was his custom, he was looking Mrs. Barrington over in the minute and yet abstracted fashion which was peculiar to him. Not for the first time I noted that when he chooses, Holmes has a disarming way with women through which he very readily establishes terms of confidence with them.

The time came to obtain a detailed account of her husband's disappearance. Mrs. Barrington rose. She led us through imposing double doors into a library or man's study, distant from prying eyes or ears. She gestured graciously to quintessentially English, leather-upholstered chesterfield chairs. Within arm's reach lay a tin of cigarettes. Holmes leaned forward and took one. She turned her luminous eyes upon me.

'And you, sir, a cigarette? I can recommend them, for my husband has them specially prepared by Ionides of Alexandria. We keep them for connoisseurs like Mr. Holmes though Captain Barrington could hardly have expected such an eminent—'

Her eyes moistened. Her voice died away in a beautiful cadence. She held out her hands as in supplication, compelling my respect and admiration. In spite of all her distraction there was a nobility in her bearing, a gallantry in the defiant chin and upraised head.

Prompted by our keen expressions, our hostess began to relate the circumstances of her husband's disappearance, how he frequently rose early to exercise his favourite horse in the forests on the lower slopes of Mount Vitosh, always returning by dusk.

Mrs. Barrington turned to address me. 'I believe you are most knowledgeable on horses, Dr. Watson? The horse in the photograph is my husband's favourite. His name is Brigadier. We brought him back from England. He's the one my husband was on when he left for the forest.'

I had taken note of Brigadier. He was a Haflinger, a well-muscled new breed, rich, golden chestnut in colour, with a refined head and light poll and a notable Arabian influence.

'A fine choice of horse for mountainous terrain,' I remarked.

My eyes drifted across to a large painting in oil on a gessoed poplar panel, signed by the greatest portrait painter of our time, the American John Singer Sargent.

Mrs. Barrington followed my gaze. 'There too, you see me with my husband.' She gestured. 'And Brigadier.'

With her assent Holmes and I got back on our feet and went to the painting. Mrs. Barrington was depicted standing on a swathe of grass. She wore an ivory-white Persian dress and a white and green over-jacket, with a turban entwined with pearls.

Her hair tumbled down her back from under it. Her smile, which we were not often to see, was striking. As though just put down, at her feet was a *sarod*, a musical instrument I had last heard strummed in a Kashmiri village. At her side, in lean silhouette, stood the missing husband, not tall but patrician in stance, once again in the full dress uniform of a Captain in the Connaught Rangers. The luxuriant black mustachios sprang out, so real I felt I could reach into the painting and twirl them.

My comrade produced a strong lens and leant into the painting to examine the Captain's face with great intensity. What had attracted his ever-active attention, I wondered?

'And this was painted when?' he asked.

'Just under a year ago,' came the reply. 'A wedding anniversary gift from the *Knyaz*.'

Holmes stood back and pointed from the painting to our hostess's hair. 'And the fine pair of diamond swallows in your hair, a family heirloom I presume?'

'Not an heirloom,' Mrs. Barrington responded.

'What then, may I enquire?' Holmes pursued.

'Also a gift from the *Knyaz*. I have heard they were given to him by the Viennese actress Kathi Schratt.'

We returned to the sofa. Holmes gave Mrs. Barrington an encouraging look. 'I wonder if you might recount the events leading up to your husband's departure on this last occasion?'

She began, 'We were engaged upon our toast and coffee in the morning. A stable-boy brought a note to the house. It was marked *For Captain Barrington. Strictly Personal*. The boy had no idea who delivered it. My husband read it and burst into laughter. He tucked the note in his pocket and said, "I have been offered a dare I cannot resist. I shall tell you all about it but not now as I must hurry". I asked, "When will you be back?" He replied, "By dawn." I exclaimed, "By dawn! Can't you at least tell me what the note says?" but again he laughed and repeated, "Don't worry, you'll hear all about it tomorrow, I promise". He told me he would return with a bouquet of cyclamen picked fresh in the forests of Mount Vitosh. He gave a droll click of his heels, raised a hand in a salute, and was gone.'

She pointed at the window. 'A little later I saw him on Brigadier. He was turning the note this way and that. Then he rode off.' After a pause she said quietly, 'And he has not been seen since.'

My comrade asked, 'Has it been Captain Barrington's habit to stay away at night?'

'Never before, no,' she replied.

Overcome with curiosity, I asked, 'Is it a general custom for beautiful Bulgarian women to marry officers of the British Army?'

Mrs. Barrington blushed. 'No, I shouldn't say it was customary by any means!'

Self-consciously I glanced across at my companion. I had expected to see him hiding a growing impatience under this inconsequential narrative, but, on the contrary, he was listening with the greatest concentration of attention.

'In the possibility your marriage to an Englishman has a bearing on your husband's disappearance, could you spare the time to tell my friend and me how such a marriage took place?' Holmes requested.

'To do so I need to go back some years, to when my father was alive,' Mrs. Barrington replied. With a concerned look she added, 'It is a story of some complexity. I—I do not know if you—?'

'Our time is entirely at your disposal,' Holmes smiled reassuringly.

She began, 'Our estates are so extensive it is said that one farm cannot see the chimney-smoke of another. My father owned more than a hundred thousand hectares of fertile lands and woods here in Bulgaria, and additional lands and villages in France, and Hungary, and elsewhere, I am told, much of which I have not seen.' She paused. 'And the story concerns a certain relative of mine. I believe you have met him.'

'And who might that be?' Holmes enquired.

'He is one of the Prince's chiefest lights, the War Minister.'

'Colonel Kalchoff!' I exclaimed, vividly recalling Mycroft's cautionary words.

'Yes. My family name is also Kalchoff. Konstantin is my cousin. He exerts himself at every turn to thwart my duties towards my estates.'

'In what way do your family estates concern your cousin, may we ask?' Holmes said.

'His father and my father were brothers. Konstantin's was the elder of the two. He predeceased my father by some years. If Konstantin had not been illegitimate he would have inherited all the Kalchoff lands. His desire to regain them quickly grew into an obsession. You may imagine my father's relief when Konstantin left Sofia for Vienna to join the Austro-Hungarian Army. That was where he became excellent friends with a certain fellow Lieutenant.'

'Would that be Prince Ferdinand?' I enquired.

She nodded. 'Some time passed peacefully, then, out of the blue, the previous *Knyaz* of Bulgaria was kidnapped and taken into exile by agents of the Russian Tsar. You can imagine our surprise when we heard Konstantin had successfully put Ferdinand's name forward for election by the *Grand Sobranje*. My cousin returned in triumph to Sofia alongside the new Prince Regnant.'

'And the matter of marrying an Englishman is in some way connected to this?' I prompted.

'My father was very friendly with the British Legate. Sir Penderel assured us that just as Ferdinand's rule is the more safeguarded from outside intervention because he is a cousin of your Queen Victoria, so our family lands could be safeguarded from Konstantin—that is, my father and Sir Penderel were both convinced only through—' Her voice faltered. 'My father was certain that my cousin could now wage a vendetta as powerful as that of any Macedonian to regain the lands which he felt were his birthright, unless—'

'Unless you married an Englishman?' I interjected.

She nodded. 'My mother died many years ago. Papa realised he would never have a son to inherit the family lands. He became impatient. "My daughter, as a woman you are very vulnerable," he told me. "You must go to England. The matter of your marriage is the greatest concern of my last days on Earth. If you are not married to an Englishman by the day I die your cousin will steal our lands from you. Do not believe the Prince Regnant will safeguard you, rather he will aid and abet Konstantin".'

Mrs. Barrington's delicate white hand pointed over her shoulder at a copy of Kelly's *Handbook to the Titled, Landed and Official Classes* standing alone on a tiny shelf.

'Evening after evening I would watch my father turning the pages of the gazette you see behind me. He marked out the names of potential suitors. By then it was becoming clear he was gravely ill.'

'And we must assume Captain Barrington was among the names,' Holmes remarked. 'Watson and I would find it of the utmost interest to know how you went about it.'

'Again I have the British Legate to thank,' Mrs. Barrington continued. 'The English hunting season was under way. Sir Penderel told us there was no quicker way for ambitious young Military officers like Captain Barrington to achieve social ascendancy, even presentation at the British Court, than cutting a good figure at a famous Hunt. He said such men move heaven and earth to get to Mr. Fernie's Billesdon Hunt at Market Harborough, its coverts venerated as the finest hunting in the world. Sir Penderel assured us that a personal invitation from Mr. Fernie, the Master of the Hunt, would soon follow if I wished to attend.'

After a reflective pause she resumed, 'My father's mind was made up. I was to leave for England as soon as I could be furnished with a suitable wardrobe.'

Our hostess laughed for the first time. 'As you may already have noticed, there is no fashion in Sofia except those we emulate from the fine people of Paris, Pesth or Vienna. I studied the fashions in the latest *La Mode Illustrée* from Paris and *Ladies Realm* from London. Then I took my choices to the Sultana's dressmaker in Stamboul.'

'And now you were ready for England and Market Harborough,' Holmes broke in, steering her back on track.

"Sir Penderel took up my family's endeavour with the greatest seriousness. He arranged for me to stay at the Ritz where a Mrs. Wheatley, a widow and distant cousin of his, would meet me each day to act as chaperone so I had a woman's countenance on my visit. I needed to spend some days in London to get fitted for a Busvine riding habit if I were to appear at the Hunt. Many times I determined to catch the next train home to Sofia but I knew I had to honour the last request my dearest Papa would ever make. My only escape was in the evenings. My chaperone and her brother, Mr. Penderel, escorted me to your wonderful theatres and concert-halls. They transported me away from all my cares.' She smiled. 'However, when I wanted to visit a music hall as I had heard much of them, Mr. Penderel refused me my request outright.'

I asked, guessing at the probable reply, 'And what was his reasoning behind this refusal?'

'He told me it was *infra dig* for a woman of my—' Again she blushed, '—class, even a foreigner!'

Holmes asked, 'Was there any particular Hall you wished to attend?'

'Why should you want to know that, Mr. Holmes?' our hostess cried, astonished.

My friend could not restrain a chuckle at her confusion. 'I am always glad of details,' he remarked, 'whether they seem to be relevant or not.' He waved a hand in my direction. 'You have a fellow enthusiast in my friend Dr. Watson. He does the rounds of all the music halls.'

'The Tivoli,' came her answer.

'And this was when precisely?' Holmes asked.

'Why, it must now be two years ago.'

'Early April?'

'Yes.'

Holmes nodded. 'Please continue.'

'To make myself—' again she blushed in a most attractive way, '—visible against all the competition, I was told to bind my hair up to show the nape of the neck, the veil should press on my face, liquid red on the lips. I exchanged the tall hat for an exotic turban tied tightly to avoid snagging on a passing branch if the pace got hectic. When my outfit was complete I hired a trap and set off for a hunting box on the Bowden Road with Mr. Penderel, himself an accomplished rider to hounds. They introduced me to Mr. Fernie. And thus the Season began for me.'

'And that's where you met and married Captain Barrington?' I summed up.

She inclined her head.

'If I may put this as delicately as possible, has a search been made in police stations and morgues for a body resembling his?' It was I who asked this question.

Again she inclined her head. 'All yesterday,' she replied. A small tear ran down her face. We rose to our feet.

'One last thing,' I said. 'Barrington is not an unusual name. There are to my knowledge half a dozen Captain Barringtons in England. In which regiment did he serve?'

'The Connaught Rangers.'

With only the greatest difficulty I prevented my jaw from dropping. I stared at her sorrowing face.

'The Connaught Rangers!' I exclaimed. 'But—'

Holmes's arm jerked sharply across my face. 'Watson, I think we have enquired enough for the moment. For our hostess's sake we must hasten this interview to an end.'

He turned to her with a slight bow. 'Madam, I assure you we shall do our very best to discover the whereabouts of your husband.'

She rose from her chair with a little of the anxiety seeping from her face. My companion continued, 'We shall take the wedding photograph with us, as you suggest. There is just one small favour I must ask of you.'

'A favour? Whatever you wish.'

'My good friend here made a small wager during our journey to your shores. I swore the Great British statesman William Ewart Gladstone was born in 1810. Watson had the temerity to insist it was 1809. I wonder if I may look quickly in your Kelly's *Handbook* to settle which of us owes the other five guineas?'

Our hostess handed him the Kelly's. Shaking his head ruefully he looked across and me and said, 'Watson, you lucky devil. You are right. He was born in 1809.'

We moved towards the door. As we reached it, our hostess said, 'My heart is lightened already since I have confided my trouble to you.'

Holmes turned once more as though to bow us out. Instead he asked, 'Mrs. Barrington, in the unavoidable absence of your father, who performed his role at the wedding?'

'Luckily, even at such short notice, an officer in the 3rd battalion of the Coldstream Guards offered to give me away.'

'His name?'

'Lieutenant-Colonel James Grant.'

***

We waited outside the villa while a servant went to summon our vehicle. I seized my comrade by the arm. In an urgent whisper I said, 'Holmes, what in heaven's name is going on? The man she says she married—Captain Barrington of the Connaught Rangers—died in a hunting accident nearly four years ago. As to the man chosen to stand in her father's place, it was announced in the *Military Gazette* that James Grant of the Coldstream Guards was the first British officer to die at the Battle of Kraaipand.'

Holmes looked grim. 'I think we can say she underwent a rather unusual ceremony. There cannot be that many weddings—even among Bulgarians—where a bride is given away to a dead man—by a dead man.'

His brow furrowed. He went on, 'A great deal of thread is piling up but I can't get the end of it into my hand. Tell me, we were offered cigarettes but why nothing from the tantalus containing brandy and whisky?'

'Holmes,' I replied, 'you are mistaken. Our hostess could not have offered us brandy or whisky from a tantalus. There was no such decanter present.'

'What of gins, vermouths and kirsches in crystal ewers?'

Again I shook my head. 'I saw only liquorice and almond emulsion. And what looked like the crimson of grenadine and garnett bitters.'

'No long-necked carafes of the mysterious and sinful drinks beloved of the Officers' Mess? Judging by the stains on your Mess Dress jacket, Army captains tend to the riotous.'

'My dear Holmes,' I retorted hotly, 'I purchased that Mess Dress from the estate of the great explorer Arthur Conolly of the 1st Bengal Light Cavalry. Those stains you refer to so disparagingly are from the finest champagne!'

'You make my point, Watson. But please answer my question, you saw no Devil's brew of any sort?'

'A milky *Advokaats*, nothing more. What are you making of this, Holmes?' I pursued.

'Just as the presence of a kennel presupposes that of a dog, so the presence of a tantalus would indicate a steady supply of Regimental comrades, and by contrast its lack would—'

He looked at me pensively. What did you make of her interest in the music hall?'

'What of it?' I asked, surprised. 'She isn't English. She might not know the Hall is nowhere for a lady to go—.'

'I find it hard to believe that she would be so interested. Such sheet music as could make it to Sofia would hardly have entranced her—ribaldry about drink, debt, adversity, lodgers, overdue rent and bailiffs, mothers-in-law, hen-pecked husbands, unfaithful wives.'

The carriage drew up. As I clambered in, I asked, 'What was all this nonsense about a bet on Gladstone's date of birth?'

'A ruse to get my hands on the Kelly's *Handbook*. I wanted to know which edition her father consulted.'

'Which was?'

'It was published in 1895.'

'Ah! Therefore—'

'—by consulting the 1895 edition she and her father would reasonably have expected Barrington to be alive.'

'So too the man she says gave her away.'

'Exactly.'

'Then how do you explain her marriage?'

'Perhaps she married a charlatan. Heaven knows the fast set also turns out in numbers at Market Harborough—a hundred predatory males and females on the make.'

'Why, Holmes,' I exclaimed, outraged, 'the utter cad!' I shook my head angrily.

'I am beginning to think that if something unpleasant has happened to this fellow, he deserves it. I suggest we return immediately to Mrs. Barrington and reveal his damnable trickery to her. What do you say?'

Holmes shook his head.

'Patience, Watson, is what I say. One hardly likes to throw suspicion where there are no proofs. This promises to be one of the more curious cases in our long career together. It certainly presents more features of interest and more possibility of development than I had originally thought. I see some light in the darkness, but it may possibly flicker out. When I compared Captain Barrington's face in the wedding photograph with Captain Barrington's face in the Sargent painting I noted something singular. The facts are, to the best of my belief, even more unusual than the matter you described in your overblown way in *The Red-Headed League.*'

CHAPTER XV
IN WHICH A BODY IS DISCOVERED

OUTSIDE the Barringtons' villa, Holmes was about to step into our conveyance when matters took a further unexpected twist. Footfalls of someone in a great hurry came to our ears. The sound was accompanied by loud sobs. A woman was rushing towards the villa entrance. Without hesitation I leapt down from the carriage and fell in with Holmes at a jog behind her.

As she entered the villa she cried out, 'Madam, Madam—a body has been found!'

Mrs. Barrington hurried from the sitting-room in alarm.

'A body!' she repeated. 'Gentlemen,' she added, catching sight of us, 'this is my housekeeper. We have taught her English for my husband's sake.'

'A body, Madam,' the housekeeper confirmed.

'Found where?' Mrs. Barrington demanded.

'In the Mount Vitosh forest. Near an *obrok*.'

For several seconds Mrs. Barrington stared in silence at the bearer of the terrible news.

'Has it been identified?' she asked finally. 'Is it—my husband?'

'No, Madam, it cannot be Captain Barrington.'

'Why so?'

'It is not a man—'

'Then a boy?'

'Not a man nor a boy.'

The three of us stared, waiting while the housekeeper drew in another agonised breath.

The woman continued, 'She has been stripped of all her clothing!'

Our hostess gasped. '*She?*'

'Yes, Madam. It is the body of a woman, a young woman hardly older than yourself! How she came there or how she met her fate are questions which are still involved in mystery. And the most terrible thing of all—'

The housekeeper gulped for breath. She brought her hands up to her ears with a shiver of horror as though to shut out the words she was about to utter.

'What terrible thing?' Mrs. Barrington demanded, her hands also beginning to rise. 'Tell me quickly!'

'The charcoal burners say that unlucky birds have been seen flocking to that part of the forest. They say the killing is the work of a vampire recently arrived. The old women have sent for the relics of Saint Ivan Rilski to exorcise the evil creature which did this dreadful thing.'

'Why should they think it was a vampire?' our hostess cried out, a quiver in her voice.

The housekeeper crooked her middle- and fore-finger and darted them at her throat.

'Her body was completely drained of blood.'

The voice portrayed the housekeeper's mind-shattering terror. She managed to gasp, 'They say her eyes still glow with a baleful light. And—'

'And *what*? Tell us at once!' our hostess demanded.

'The vampire cut off all her hair,' the woman replied hoarsely. 'The woman was shorn just like a sheep.'

Our hostess turned white to her very lips. She stood petrified for a moment. Before I could take three short paces to her side she fell to the floor in a deep faint.

CHAPTER XVI
THE VICTIM OF A VAMPIRE?

WITH the application of volatile salts Mrs. Barrington opened her eyes. She looked up at me beseechingly.

'Dr. Watson, you are a medical man. You must go at once with my housekeeper to Mount Vitosh. You can make enquiry of the villagers. Perhaps the woman is not quite dead. As to the peasants, for some weeks they have been insisting a voracious vampire has recently been driven into the forests of Mount Vitosh from the region of Istria, but a prudent incredulity is very requisite.'

'Madam, may I ask what is an *obrok*?' I enquired.

'A shrine. The villagers offer sacrificial rituals to their patron saint against evil spirits who live in the forest. An ancient tree over an *obrok* is considered sacred. The hollows and cracks become resting places for the black stork and bats. But hurry, please hurry, in case she is still alive!'

The housekeeper rushed away. She returned ready for the forest in a dolman cape and elastic-sided boots. At Holmes's prompting, I scribbled a hurried note for our driver to deliver to the Legate and we sent the phaeton back. We followed the housekeeper towards a conveyance belonging to the Estate. A post-boy hurried from the stables and mounted one of the three drawing horses.

Along our route little groups of aproned women huddled at their doorways. Frightened villagers urged us onward along steeper and steeper trails blazed through the forest. Mount Vitosh loomed before us like a menacing cloud of episcopal violet against the golden sky. We were entering a world of un-things: mist, ghosts, shrouds, gossamer, smoke. I felt a creeping of the flesh, and a presentiment of coming horror. My nerves, which were steady enough on the field of battle, tingled. The horses, nostrils flaring like the great horses of the Parthenon, drove us onward through sharp, dead limbs between which there was hardly room to pass, into the gloom of a dense, ancient forest otherwise silent except for the horses' shrill breath and the snap of decaying timber. Suddenly we broke into a lovely glade of greensward.

There are sights such as meet the eye which etch lines on the mind so deep that our memory stays dominated by them until we move to the Great Beyond. The lapse of eighteen years has hardly served to weaken the effect. The dead woman lay on her back, seeming to spring from the roots of a great pedunculate oak. Her naked body gave the appearance of being hewn from the finest alabaster, the hands stretched half away from her body as though ready to fly. The clothing was nowhere to be seen. Frighteningly, the bifurcation gave her the appearance of the human-shaped root of the Chinese fleece-flower so familiar in the East.

Three men with flintlock rifles stood at the edge of the clearing, ill-at-ease, their horses tethered nearby. The housekeeper offered them an explanation for our presence and translated their response. The older of the three called across, 'Tell the doctor to hurry with his business, then we can stake her through the heart and hip.' Another nodded in agreement, adding, 'Approach the undead with care—she may return to life at any second.'

My comrade acknowledged their concern with a wave of a hand. He set about inspecting the ground around the corpse. 'She put up a struggle,' he said quietly, pointing to the disturbances around the body. Her missing footwear had repeatedly dug and twisted into the soil in a desperate effort to throw off a heavy weight. Deeper, sharper furrows interspersed her heel marks.

After a few minutes Holmes beckoned me to examine her. I kneeled by the corpse and stared at her face. The features were contorted. A thick layer of cosmetic had run between her eyebrows and her eyes, staining the sclera yellow. A small mirror held to her mouth and nostrils showed no sign of breath. I lifted her chin to examine her throat.

'Well, Holmes,' I said, standing up. 'I'm afraid she's very much dead. There's no need to sniff her lips for poison. Facial petechiæ erythema around the neck and involuntary defecation all indicate strangulation, but the cause of death was exsanguination. There isn't a drop of blood left in her. There are two fang-like punctures on the left side of her neck just below the chin but the one slash which divided the carotid artery would have sufficed.'

I threw Holmes a troubled look. 'I have heard that vampires first strangle their victims before they suck out their blood. This poor woman was certainly strangled, but it was not a pair of fangs which punctured the artery. Her murderer used a sharp blade.'

Holmes remarked, 'He must have been strong to have overpowered her so quickly—there is no sign of a paralysing blow—and he would have been well-known to her.'

'How do you deduce that, Holmes?'

'It has long been an axiom of mine that the little things are infinitely the most important. Great issues may hang from a boot-lace.' He gestured towards the corpse's lower trunk. 'Impoverished forest-dwellers might pillage riding-boots or a hunting habit and sandwich box, but I doubt if they would take away soiled underwear. Why was someone so anxious to get possession of it? There must be some strong reason behind the removal, that even that one piece of clothing could disclose the victim's identity and point us towards her killer. However, he has left us a clue. He is at least six feet tall, to judge by the marks of his boot-toes in the soil—they are several inches below the furrows made by the dead woman's heels, and she is about five feet six inches in height.'

'I can offer you a further clue, Holmes,' I intervened.

'Which is?'

'The face which pressed hard against hers during the struggle was ill-shaven or bearded. Her cheeks have been considerably abraded.'

'Excellent, Watson,' Holmes returned. 'And what of her missing hair?'

'Quite clearly the villain was a fetishist, Holmes. Many people become aroused by human hair. This would be even more likely if it was raining at the time and the hair was soaking wet.'

'Perhaps,' Holmes replied. 'Trichophilia is a possibility but why not one strand or tuft of hair on the ground—not even in the halo of congealed blood around her head? As we are in the Balkans we must follow Mrs. Barrington's excellent counsel, which you recall was—?'

'A "prudent incredulity" is very requisite,' I replied.

'The body must return with us, even if we pay with the Prince's gold *leva* for the privilege—otherwise—' He gestured in silent eloquence towards the waiting men.

'What of motive, Holmes?' I asked, beckoning the housekeeper over. 'I see no signs of injury elsewhere upon the body to indicate indecent assault. Apart from the theft of her clothes—and hair—there is not a ghost of a motive anyone can suggest.'

My companion made no response to my query. He pointed to a small patch of flattened grass. In a curiously distrait tone he said, 'Her murderer sat watching while she bled to death. Few killers in our lexicon of crime have displayed such cruelty and calculation as this.' He threw me a determined look. 'Watson, I swear he shall face the hangman's noose.'

CHAPTER XVII
A SHOCKING SPECTACLE

THE following day the Capital's newspapers were filled with villagers' wildly exaggerated accounts of the bizarre murder, replete with wood-cuts of vampires and a painting by Burne-Jones. In an attempt to prevent the vampire moving across the Danube, the Patriarch of Rumania intended to offer a special Divine Liturgy in the Archiepiscopal Cathedral of Galati to invoke St. Andrew, patron of wolves and donor of garlic. In Sofia the three men at the glade gave evidence at a quickly convened deposition. They affirmed on oath that when they arrived at the glade a crescent moon above them grew full in seconds and turned blood red. They swore that before the two strangers came and took the dead body away it had twice jumped eight feet off the ground and flown at their throats in a desperate effort to replace its lost blood. In flight little points of light floated in the air around it. Its eyes had emitted a yellow glow.

Bulgaria's high society was agog. The custom among the wealthy of riding for pleasure in the Mount Vitosh foot-hills in the cool of the morning fell dramatically from favour. Mass hysteria infected the countryside. Mustard seed was sprinkled on every roof-top. Sales of apotropaics, traditionally high, soared even higher. Merchants ran out of garlic by mid-day. As during previous vampire outbreaks, villagers fled their houses and slept clumped together in one building, rubbing garlic on every door and window. Even though a post-mortem had quickly concluded she was still a virgin, there was lurid speculation on whether the vampire had inseminated the corpse which might then—even after burial—give birth to a *dzhadadzhiya*, the child of a vampire and human mother.

Fearing the woman's death heralded the return of a vampire epidemic, regional groups were forming, prepared to fight a long-running battle against further undead who, galvanised by the events in the Mount Vitosh forest, even now would be sharpening their teeth and twisting and turning and stretching in their graves like fledging corvids.

In an effort to reassure and calm the public, the Prince ordered a coffin decked in silk crape. The corpse was to await identification under twenty-four-hour armed guard in the Coburg family mausoleum in Sofia. If no one came forward it would be taken to a crematorium and burnt to cinders over a cleansing bonfire of wild rose and hawthorn plants. At the Prince's suggestion, the ashes would be taken to Philippopolis, the city founded by the father of Alexander the Great, and provided with a final resting place in the Church of St. Louis, thus held captive for ever in holy ground.

In the late afternoon a smart landau and pair of greys sent by the British Legation arrived at the Panachoff to take us to the Royal Command performance of *Salomé*. As we clambered aboard, Holmes cocked a quizzical eye at me. 'Doctor,' he said, 'What's the matter? You're not looking quite yourself. The woman's murder has upset you?'

'To tell the truth, it has,' I confirmed. 'It reminds me of the dark incidents in *A Study In Scarlet* and makes me just as uneasy. I ought to be more case-hardened after my Afghan experiences with so many stinking dead. I saw my own comrades hacked to pieces at Maiwand. I felt no touch of fear upon those occasions.

'I can understand,' came the sympathetic reply. 'There is a mystery about this case which stimulates the imagination; where there is no imagination there is no horror.'

When the carriage pulled away I asked, 'Holmes, more to the point, what do you think has happened to Captain Barrington?

Not a hint of his whereabouts has been reported. With your wonderful capacity to reason, I am confident you will soon arrive at the truth.'

'I am coming to the conclusion,' Holmes replied soberly, 'that some unforeseen catastrophe has occurred to him. As to the truth—I wonder. We must always consider that the purpose of human reason may not be to find truth but simply to persuade other people that we're right.'

***

Sir Penderel was waiting for us at the theatre, a Moorish style edifice with lavish fenestration, two towers and a dome, of a solemnity and luxury already going from fashion in the rest of Europe. He led us up wide stairs to the Legation box immediately adjacent to one packed to the gunnels with the Prince's *camarilla*, including Colonel Kalchoff and two or three young Army officers. At their side sat several women aglitter with necklaces, brooches, bracelets and trinkets, crowned by the curls and loops in which they dressed their hair. The provocative smell of carnation perfume drifted across to our seats. Soldiers like flying ants combed the ceiling and proscenium for explosives. A small orchestra was tuning up, consisting mainly of the Gypsy musicians from the Sherlock Holmes competition.

Several rows of seats in the Stalls had been removed to make way for gilded armchairs sent from the Palace. Ferdinand and a large retinue made an entrance. The Prince bowed to the invited audience, turning his head upwards to nod in friendly fashion at Sir Penderel, with a further, more solemn nod to us. The theatre hushed. A short delay ensued while the soldiers came down from the proscenium stage to probe the padding of the armchairs for bombs or other murderous engines. The *Knyaz* took his seat.

At the faint sound of flute and zither rising up from the pit, the curtain rose on an exotic scene outside Herod's palace. Copper bowls and ewers and enormous silver cups lay scattered around the stage. Salomé appeared, pale-faced, almost immaterial, with appealing, wild black eyes and scarlet lips. She stood as though frozen in ice, an iridescent mass of silks and ostrich feathers. Her train gleamed like stained glass in the moonlight, adorned with countless blue foil and velvet butterflies. Now with the slow, formal gestures of a sorceress, now with the cuffing movement of a cat playing with a doomed mouse, Salomé began to taunt a roped John The Baptist, her eyes fixed on the lower half of his agonised face.

'Iokanaan, it is thy mouth that I desire. Thy mouth is like a band of scarlet on a tower of ivory. It is like a pomegranate cut in twain with a knife of ivory. The pomegranate flowers that blossom in the gardens of Tyre, and are redder than roses, are not so red. The red blasts of trumpets that herald the approach of kings, and make afraid the enemy, are not so red—'

Her head leaned forward towards him like a heron about to strike. 'There is nothing in the world so red as thy mouth. Suffer me to kiss thy mouth.' She reared back. 'What! You have nothing to say! You reject me! Yet I say, I will kiss thy mouth, Iokanaan. I—will—kiss—thy—mouth.'

The curtain fell.

When it rose, the shockingly young Salomé stood alone on the stage. A servant came in, bearing the Baptist's head on a silver platter. Blood dripped profusely from it. Salomé seized the severed head by the black matted hair and dangled it in front of her, addressing the sightless eyes.

'Ah! Thou wouldst not suffer me to kiss thy mouth. Well! I will kiss it now. I will bite it with my teeth as one bites a ripe fruit. Yes, I will kiss thy mouth.'

As she uttered the words a spurt of blood burst from the severed neck and spattered down to the floorboards. She twisted and turned, kneading the blood into the stage as though pressing grapes. The crimson smeared into a circle hardly wider than her small feet.

'I said it; did I not say it?' Salomé remonstrated. 'I said it. Ah! I will kiss it now. But wherefore dost thou not look at me? Thine eyes that were so terrible, so full of rage and scorn are shut now. Wherefore are they shut? Open thine eyes! Lift up thine eyelids!'

I began to feel in need of air, overcome by the same nausea I experienced on the choppy sea-crossing to France. I started to rise, whispering an apology to an entranced Sir Penderel. Holmes's hand restrained me.

'Hold hard, Watson, there is something here—' he cautioned in an urgent whisper.

I returned my eyes to the stage. The slight, beautiful Salomé with her tea-rose skin stood there motionless. She brought the still-bleeding head closer and closer to her face, the gap narrowing inch by inch until suddenly, unbelievably, the two mouths met. A shocked silence engulfed the theatre. Seconds passed while she held the Baptist's mouth hard against hers as though her young lips were wrestling a spirit from it. After an age, the pairs of lips pulled slowly apart.

'Ah!' she called out wildly to the severed head. 'John, I have kissed thy mouth, I have kissed thy mouth. There was a bitter taste on thy lips. Was it the taste of blood? Nay; but perchance it was the taste of love. They say that love hath a bitter taste. But what matter? What matter? I have kissed thy mouth.'

The curtain fell. Applause led by the Prince began. Holmes grabbed my arm, his voice cutting through the sound.

'Watson! Now we must go—and faster than the wind. Sir Penderel, forgive us, for we must leave you.'

I caught a glimpse of Colonel Kalchoff leaning forward, his expression startled as he observed our precipitate exit. We rattled down the long flight of stairs, my comrade's eyes shining, his cheeks tinged with colour. Only at a crisis have I seen those battle-signals flying.

'What is it, Holmes?' I called out as I puffed after him in great confusion.

He called back, 'I deserve to be kicked from here to Charing Cross. Salomé has given us the very answer we have been seeking!'

Chapter XVIII
SALOMÉ GIVES HOLMES THE CLUE

OUTSIDE the theatre, we searched for a public conveyance. Almost invisible in the confusion of ostlers rubbing down matched carriage-horses were two conveyances on offer, the one a jolting Droshky, the other a tall *chaise à porteurs*, two tunnels of yellow light spilling out from its side lanterns. Holmes led me into the chaise, drew up the windows against the cold night air, tapped on the wood-work, and with a flick of their heels, the porters whirled us away through the darkness. Soon we were trotting into an endless succession of covered bridges and melancholy, deserted streets, silent and lifeless as some city in a dream. Not even the clatter of a piano resounded through the night.

'Holmes,' I begged. 'Please let me know what we are up to!'

'We are going to Vasil Levski Boulevard.'

His hand shot up. 'Before you ask the inevitable, my dear Watson, we must keep Mycroft's words in mind.'

'Which in particular?' I asked.

'"Nothing you take for granted in England will offer you any sort of blueprint for your stay".'

My companion gave a short laugh. 'He might well have quoted *Alice's Adventures in Wonderland*—"But I don't want to go among mad people," Alice remarked. "Oh, you can't help that," said the Cat: "we're all mad here. I'm mad. You're mad".'

I took up the familiar refrain. '"How do you know I'm mad?" said Alice'.'

To which Holmes ad-libbed, 'We must all be, or we wouldn't be here.'

I stared out at the dark streets. 'Why are we heading for Vasil Levski Boulevard?' I demanded at last.

'That's where the body of the murdered woman lies, at the Coburg Mortuary Chapel.'

'Why would you want to examine her again?' I asked, unsettled by this development.

'Other than a pair of reading-glasses, nothing affords a finer field for inference than a cadaver.'

'You say Salomé has supplied the answer we've been seeking? How so?'

'Do you remember when she drew the severed head of John the Baptist to her own?'

'Shall I ever forget it!' I exclaimed. 'Why, nothing among the Timurids—'

'And when the Baptist's grisly black hair pressed against her young face?'

'Indeed. The blood trickling through the beard! I nearly retched.'

'That triggered nothing in your mind, Watson? Come, think hard! When Salomé tore the head away and we could see her bare face again—?'

I shook my head. 'I'm sorry, Holmes, I am at a complete loss.'

After my reply, despite my importunate enquiry, he would only say, 'We need to glance a little more closely into details. It is imperative to examine the body one last time,' adding quietly, 'There lacks one final proof before we confront the killer and reveal the solution to the world.'

Following this dramatic pronouncement Holmes fell into an obdurate silence. I gave it over in despair and turned my attention to the outside world. Above us, a star or two twinkled dimly here and there through the rifts of the clouds spreading away from the volcanic peak of Mount Vitosh.

In the night, the city seemed to possess a peculiar acoustic property. Each sound was magnified, even the clink of our human horses' shoes. A solitary passing carriage sounded like the parade-ground drill of a brigade of cavalry.

Some fifteen minutes later we crossed a murky, sluggish river and came to a large square. The air was pungent with the smell of stables and rotting vegetables. Despite the elegance and spacious nature of the habitations of iron and copper mine-proprietors to every side, and those built by merchants exporting flax, linseed, honey and tallow, the atmosphere was desolate. In Sofia it seemed nearly everyone except the street-sweepers collecting up piles of horse-droppings was in bed by ten.

Unwilling to approach the Mausoleum in the gloom, the porters halted in the centre at an obelisk remarkably like the milestone in London's St. George's Circus. This one honoured the Prince's predecessor, Alexander. By it stood a small, silent coffee-stall, grey-hooded and with a pale lamp. We crossed the square on foot. The edifice was entirely surrounded by halberdiers. An officer in charge held a lantern to our faces and gave us permission to enter. My senses were already heightened by the sight of Salomé pressing her mouth to the severed head of John the Baptist. Inside they were further assaulted by the hot-house temperature, the massed flowers, the burning candles, the overpowering incense, all contained and compressed within Imperial porphyry walls.

Holmes gave a satisfied grunt. 'Ah, she is still here,' he whispered.

A single shaft of moonlight from an upper window fell upon the young woman's cadaver. Her face was mask-like. A winding-cloth covered her up to her neck. A ruche of black gauze disguised as far as possible the strikingly vivid strangulation marks. By her side lay a pair of gloves and a fan. In the candlelight her lips shone in a crimson ellipse, shaped and coloured by the art of the undertaker with cochineal dye and beeswax. No longer utterly pallid, the cheeks were now too red.

A custodian lay asleep on the floor, wearing a shabby dark brown suit of the native tweed, the black-cloth collar shiny with grease. He awoke at our entry. Noting our attire, he rose respectfully. Holmes signed to him, 'We have come to pay our respects to the dear departed', adding aloud, 'In our country, our custom is to show the utmost respect for the dead by a kiss.'

Startled, I began, 'But, Holmes—'

I was silenced by his urgent whisper: 'Not now, Watson, I beg you.' Louder, he continued to address me, 'Doctor, you may pay your respects to the dear departed in your turn, in your own way, as I must in mine.'

The man took hold of the shroud as though to throw it back to reveal a hand. 'On the lips,' Holmes repeated, illustrating his words by tapping a forefinger to his own. Reaching into his pocket as he spoke my companion brought out a gold hundred-*leva* coin. It glistered even in the dim light.

Overwhelmed by Holmes's superb assurance, the man took the gratuity with a slight, if uncertain nod, and moved across the marble floor to withdraw the rope between us and the catafalque. He pointed wordlessly to a small jewelled casket containing a chrismaria of holy oils before turning away to permit us the moment's privacy.

Holmes stepped forward. He bent over the dead woman. For a moment his face hovered over hers like a bird of prey, a gap of a mere inch between his nose and hers. In the dim light he looked more Iroquois Indian than Celt. Suddenly his head dropped down. His face pressed voraciously into the swathe of bright red colouring. His thin lips swept from side to side across her mouth like a bison wiping away snow to reach the vegetation below. That the first kiss I had ever seen delivered by the most perfect reasoning and observing machine the world has ever known should be delivered to a woman's corpse shocked me to my very essence. My legs went weak with the horror of it.

For perhaps six seconds Holmes's lips remained locked to hers before he detached himself and straightened up. He dipped a finger in the chrism and touched a small amount of the sweetened olive oil at the point the woman's nose met her forehead. The scent of balsam lifted into the heated air of the Mausoleum.

A further long minute passed. My comrade stepped away from the catafalque and turned to thank the custodian. The man's eyes widened. He gave a shriek the like of which I had never before heard from a human-being. It vibrated with a frenzy of terror in the small space enclosed by the red marble walls, reverberating across the Mausoleum until it ran together into one long unearthly scream.

Holmes turned swiftly to me. The same thrill of horror which sent the custodian fleeing suffused me. My comrade's close-set grey eyes and sharp, hawk-like nose were now conjoined with a ghastly slash of crimson which extended his mouth more than an inch to either side. He looked as if he had feasted ravenously on the dead woman's blood, as though he was now a member of the brotherhood of vampires.

These many years later I retain a vivid recollection of that instant, of Holmes' triumphant expression, the ring of his voice, his proclamation, 'The matter grows in interest. Watson, I have seen and done everything that I need to. Pay your respects if you wish and we must leave.'

Still reeling from the horror of his face, I reached down and gave a swift pull at the shroud to access the woman's hand. With the winding-cloth withdrawn, a ship's chain holding fast to her wrists and ankles became visible. The hand I intended to bring to my lips fell away with a loud clank. The authorities had made sure this unclaimed corpse was firmly pinned down by the dead weight of cast-iron. The victim of a vampire would never rise up from the dead to pursue a frightened populace.

Chapter XIX
DÉNOUEMENT

TO my immense relief Holmes led us out of the Mausoleum. We found ourselves once more on the dusty square. The halberdiers, deeply disconcerted by the custodian's headlong flight through their cordon, fell away in confusion. I chided my companion immediately. 'Holmes, kissing a dead woman on the mouth is not something I would expect—'

He interrupted me with a grim but satisfied look. 'Pshaw, Watson! I can assure you the meeting of our lips was as instructive as a meeting of our minds. I have in my hands,' he continued confidently, 'all the threads which have formed such a tangle.'

'Then I wish you would put me out of my bewilderment!' I exclaimed. 'Never in all my years with you—'

'My dear Watson,' my comrade returned, 'I do not wish to make a mystery but a little over-precipitance may ruin all. We must move with great speed, otherwise I would put you out of your misery. Soon I shall lay an account of the case before you in its due order, showing you the various points which guided me in my deduction. I merely remind you that women are naturally secretive, and they like to do their own secreting.'

I was not to be silenced. 'I have no doubt even a connection between old Army boots and a Turkish bath is perfectly self-evident to a logical mind, and yet I should be obliged if you would indicate what in the name of the Almighty could you discover by giving the cadaver so—so—*muscular* a kiss on the mouth? I would never have expected—'

'My dear sir,' Holmes broke back impatiently, 'in your time in my wake what you would never have expected would fill far more battered tin-boxes than the dozen or so shilling dreadfuls you have so far managed to scribble.' He continued in a more placatory tone, 'I tell you we are enveloped in a riddle wrapped in a mystery as deep and complex as anything we have ever confronted. Remind me, what was your explanation for the abrasions on her face?'

'Clearly the assailant's beard rubbed savagely against her cheeks,' I replied. 'What else could it be?'

'An ingenious and not entirely impossible supposition. However, I would call your attention very particularly to two points. First, why does the faint smell of mastic cling to those cheeks? Furthermore, if yours is the correct explanation, why was the light down hair one would expect on the woman's upper lip completely absent, a fact I discovered by snorting away the lavender powder and thrusting aside the lip-paint with my— as you say—muscular kiss? If you provide an explanation for those puzzling facts you have solved the riddle of the missing husband.'

'The missing husband!' I exclaimed, astounded. 'What connexion could there be between this poor woman and Captain Barrington? Are you suggesting she was his mistress— that he murdered her for fear of exposure and fled abroad?'

My comrade shook his head. 'If that were true, then the case is at an end. We could set Harker of the Central Press Syndicate on him, or the Baker Street Irregulars. Or place an advertisement in the London *Telegraph* and offer a generous reward for information on the Captain's whereabouts.'

He looked at me gravely. 'No, Watson, I say we must move with the utmost speed. I believe the life of someone you have a soft spot for is in the most imminent danger.'

'Who might that—' I asked, surprised.

'Mrs. Barrington, of course,' came the answer.

'*Mrs. Barrington?*' I repeated, gaping at my companion. 'Why should anyone want to harm—'

My companion brushed my words aside. 'Not now, Watson,' he returned. 'Tell me, that photographic contraption given to you by the Prince, the bellows camera—are you able to work its magic?'

'Certainly,' I plumed. 'Up the Grim we—'

'Then have a message delivered to the Palace tonight as follows: 'Your Highness, with the unexpected return of the Codex there is nothing to keep us any longer in your country. We intend to return to England very shortly. Before departing, Dr. Watson has a small favour to ask. Please arrange for the War Minister to pose for the camera in the caparison for which we will always remember him, as the winner of the Sherlock Holmes competition. SH'.'

I exclaimed, 'What a fine idea. What a wonderful souvenir of our time in the Balkans! I shall offer it to my Editor to accompany the adventure I plan to title *The Case of The Bulgarian Codex.*'

'As you wish. And Watson, along with the camera, do not fail to bring your service revolver.'

These words from Holmes, following close on his remark that Mrs. Barrington's life was in great danger, brought me up short. I had not up to this point taken a very serious view of the case. It seemed grotesque and bizarre rather than perilous.

While I absorbed this unexpected command, my comrade resumed, 'I have one more important task for you. Even if you have to force him from his bed this night, ask Penderel Moon to send an urgent reply-paid telegram to the manager of the Tivoli Theatre. There is a point I wish to ascertain.'

'Which is?' I asked, suspending my propelling pencil.

'Who topped the bill during the early part of April two years ago?'

* * *

The next morning the British Legation forwarded the theatre manager's reply to our hotel. I hastened telegram in hand to Holmes's room. He was seated in an alcove puffing on a large cigar, his feet thrust into red heelless Turkish slippers provided by the hotel. His back was to me as he gazed out on a cemetery. The tombs were simple flagstones level with the ground without crosses or columns or *stelae*. Scattered families sat among them in the cool air conversing with the Departed, some with little birds in cages.

Without looking round, Holmes waved me to an armchair. A hand rose over his shoulder. It pointed in the direction of a small side-table supporting several more cigars wrapped up in silver paper.

'Do try one, Watson. They are a gift from the most devious Prince in Christendom. Don't be alarmed—they don't seem to be explosive. And help yourself to a cup of tea.'

He swung the chair to look at me. 'Do I deduce from your energetic arrival and bewildered look that we have had a reply from London?'

'We have, Holmes. You wanted to know who topped the bill at the Tivoli in early April two years ago, but for the life of me I can't see—'

'—why I would take an interest in Miss Vesta Tilley?'

'Why, Holmes,' I responded, gaping at him, 'how ever did you—?'

Holmes chuckled and wriggled in his chair, a habit when in high spirits. He jumped up.

'Later, Watson, later! Drink up your tea or abandon it. We must return to Mrs. Barrington's. We are ready for the *dénouement.*'

Seated in the carriage my comrade's eyes took on the introspective look I have observed whenever he exerts his full powers. What Holmes' luminous intellect finds simple frequently bewilders me. Once again I had a sense it is not logic, cold and ordinary, which enables him to solve his cases. It is the clairvoyant's eye for detail. Of the greats of the past, the giants on whose shoulders he modestly remarks he stands, he is most like Urbain Le Verrier, the mathematician who discovered the planet Neptune and determined its dimensions long before telescopes powerful enough to pick it out in the night sky were invented. Yet in this instance Holmes seemed determined to leave me completely in the same stygian dark.

Holmes was still resisting my demands for an explanation ("You have a grand gift of silence, Watson, now is a good time to exercise it.") when we arrived at the Barrington villa. He banged at the door until the flustered housekeeper peered through a slit. Once more we were shown into the drawing-room. I waited for our hostess with a mix of trepidation and a high degree of irritation at Holmes's reticence.

Soon Mrs. Barrington made her entrance. She wore a white cashmere costume with a band of lace some four inches wide encircling her waist. She greeted us with a bob and a gesture at her attire.

'As you can see, I am hoping my husband will return at any moment,' she explained.

Her appearance contradicted her optimistic words. With the passage of a single day her eyes had grown dark with sorrow. She plumped down on the *fauteuil* where she sat looking from one of us to the other with an uncertain smile. Her expression soon turned to one of apprehension, as though our sudden appearance and especially Holmes's steadfast look had shaken her nerves.

Finally she offered, 'Shall we return to the study?' and once settled there she asked, 'You have made progress, gentlemen? Have you any news of Captain Barrington?'

Holmes responded gravely. 'We have come to tell you that half-confidences are worse than none, Mrs. Barrington. It is imperative you are absolutely frank with us. You failed to inform us of your visit to the Tivoli Theatre that early April, indeed you misled us by saying your chaperone had refused to allow you to attend. I understand why. The good Doctor here has made enquiry as to the playbill at the Tivoli at the time.'

A flush stole over Mrs. Barrington's lovely face. She burst into a storm of passionate sobbing.

'Holmes!' I ejaculated, half-rising. 'What in the name of—!' I threw him a severe look. 'You have badly hurt her feelings with your accusations!'

Deeply discomfited, I stared back and forth between the two. Several minutes went by before Mrs. Barrington regained her composure. Then Holmes said to her,

'I beg you to lay before us everything that may help us in forming an opinion upon the matter. You must tell us the truth, for there lies your only hope of safety. I must advise you any circumlocution or concealment may quickly lead to your own death.'

Her breathing grew high and thin at Holmes's ominous words. Her explanation began to flow like the bursting of a dam.

'So you have discovered the secret of Captain Barrington,' she addressed us, dabbing at her eyes.

'Apparently my good friend has,' I rejoined plaintively, 'but as yet he has kept me in ignorance. I wonder if you might be kind enough to reveal any such secret to me?'

'You have just been to the Coburg Mausoleum, have you not?' came the response.

I nodded, bewildered. 'We have, yes, but how does—'

'And you saw the body of the murdered woman lying there?'

'We did.'

'The corpse you saw there, as Mr. Holmes has deduced, is the body of my husband, Captain Barrington.'

My mouth dropped open in uncontrollable astonishment. 'Good Lord!' I exclaimed, and relapsed into a stunned silence.

Our hostess turned a dolorous gaze on my companion.

'Mr. Holmes, I beg you to listen to my explanation. I throw myself on your honour and your love of justice. If our deception is to be revealed, so be it, but first let me tell you all. You must already understand it is an unusual story and of considerable complexity.'

We listened spellbound as she unfolded an extraordinary tale. At times she spoke in a voice so low that I could hardly catch the words but as I listened the mists in my own mind gradually cleared away.

'I hope you will accept that everything my—husband—and I did was through my father's concern for our family estates. I told you his exact words—"You must go to England, my daughter. The matter of your marriage is the greatest concern of my final days. If you are not married to an Englishman most urgently, Konstantin will steal our lands when I die." I related how he chose Captain Barrington from the Kelly's *Handbook*, the name kept to ourselves and revealed to no other. I described how I prepared my wardrobe to attend Mr. Fernie's Billesdon Hunt, that I hired a box at Market Harborough and set about seeking out the eligible young Captain my father wished me to marry.'

She paused. With a strained look, she recommenced.

'At Market Harborough I was brought to the Major-General charged with introducing me to eligible officers, though not fully apprised of my goal. One by one I met them—this is Lieutenant So-and-so, this is Captain So-and-so. None of them bore the name Barrington. Finally, at lunch, I mentioned Captain Barrington by name.

The Major-General looked startled. "Captain Barrington?" "Yes," I replied. "Of the Connaught Rangers?" he asked. I confirmed this was so. He said, "I am sorry to tell you that he is no longer among the living". You can imagine my horror!' our hostess exclaimed, gulping in her throat to keep down her agitation.

She continued, 'I asked him, "Was it from wounds he received in the Matabele War?" "No, he survived Africa and returned home," he replied, "only to kill himself in a riding accident back here".'

Mrs. Barrington looked at us beseechingly. 'Imagine my plight. I must marry within days, only to discover the man my father had selected, the rescuer whose mercy I intended to beg, the man I hoped would consent to enter into marriage with me and oversee our family estates in Bulgaria and Hungary—was dead. I determined to leave Market Harborough the very next morning. I would send Mrs. Wheatley and her brother away, and return to Sofia, my whole mission an abject failure.

I left the lunch-table in tears. I had let down my dying father. I had failed the family estates. Unless I found a husband within the remaining hours of my father's life, Konstantin would make a sudden move to seize everything. By now the huntsmen and the followers were flashing out in pursuit of a fox. Mr. Penderel led me outside where I mounted and followed. Soon, though, he had ridden ahead. A young Englishwoman with beautiful golden hair rode up to me. She told me her name was Julia. She had been looking for me. At the Major-General's command, she was to stay with me during the afternoon. The Major-General himself no longer rode to hounds all day. He knew Mr. Penderel would be tempted by the fox and not remain at my side.'

Our hostess emitted a deep sigh. 'Julia asked why I was so distressed. I poured out my heart to her. I explained why the matter was so urgent, how I could lose my estates to Konstantin. I told her I could stand this strain no longer; I should go mad if it continued. I translated into English the telegram which arrived that very morning from my family's Land Agent telling me my father had but days to live, and would die without peace of mind unless I married without delay. I told her how Papa had chosen an English captain from Kelly's *Handbook*, that I had come specially to Market Harborough to hunt for a husband rather than a fox, how horrified I had been when the Major-General told me Captain Barrington was dead.'

Our hostess paused to allow us to absorb the depths of her predicament.

'And that was when she suggested you meet up in London?' Holmes prompted.

Mrs. Barrington nodded. 'Julia said she had an idea. She asked if I would return to London and accompany her to the Tivoli theatre the next evening, disguised and without a chaperone at my side. I agreed. We met in the foyer. She had been thinking hard about my situation. She told me she was intimately acquainted with someone I should marry, who would be willing to do so on the instant. I asked, "Who might that be? Is he an officer?" and she laughed, and said, "He could be—but wait until we have watched this evening's performance". We took our seats and very shortly bounding on to the stage was this handsome dandy, Burlington Bertie of Bow, singing *The Latest Chap on Earth.*'

Our hostess's face lit up. She put her head up and in a delightful voice sang "He has the latest thing in collars, the latest thing in ties, The latest specimen of girly girls with the latest blue, blue eyes".

'And you had no idea Burlington Bertie was a male impersonator?' I asked, unable to prevent myself laughing.

'No idea at all,' came the embarrassed reply. 'The performance was without the slightest hint of grotesqueness or vulgarity. I knew nothing of male impersonators, and nothing about the famous Miss Tilley.'

'Do continue,' I begged.

'When the performance came to an end I turned to Julia and said, "Now you must tell me your idea—tell me who will become my husband. How can you be certain that he will say yes?" At which she put an arm around my shoulder, looked straight into my eyes and said: "You are to marry *me!*"

"*You!*" I exclaimed.

"Yes, me. For your father's sake. And to preserve your estates. It's clear Captain Barrington is entirely unknown in Bulgaria. I shall become Captain Barrington. I have no family and I had intended to go to America to seek my fortune. No one will miss me. We shall only have to pretend for a year or two to stave off your cousin while you take full command of your estates." And she added with a further laugh, "Then we can obtain a divorce".

I was about to express my incredulity when she pointed towards the stage and said, "I know Burlington Bertie. He has invited us to go to his dressing-room".

Without a further word she led me back-stage. Burlington Bertie—that is to say, Miss Tilley—grasped my cause immediately. The next morning she sent us to a military tailor to purchase a fine uniform. We spent the next few days with Miss Tilley while she taught Julia how to dress and act like a man.'

For several minutes Mrs. Barrington entertained us with the instruction her husband-to-be received from the great impersonator; how they purchased a close-cut black wig brushed straight back, pomaded with macassar oil; how Julia was taught to thicken her eyebrows with the eye-shadow and mascara used on the stage, and how to employ spirit gum ('Here in Bulgaria we make use of mastic') to hold a false beard or moustache in place, and how to develop masculine gestures and decisive, crisp movements.

Our hostess continued, 'Finally we were sent to addresses in Soho to buy Julia's compression shirts and built-up footwear, and to commission a pair of dyed-black mustachios, woven by skilled artisans from her own hair, to which by now I had taken my scissors. We emerged from the back of the Theatre to promenade up Regent Street and Portland Place to the Regent's Park, Julia clad in her Captain's uniform or one of Miss Tilley's beautifully-tailored Savile Row suits, sporting the new mustachios.'

'And no one gave you the slightest indication they considered you anything else but man and wife?' I ventured.

'Not one soul,' she replied.

I asked, 'And it was your idea that your husband-to-be should wear such mustachios because the Prince Regnant wears them?'

'As you say, Dr. Watson. Like your Prince of Wales and his Homburg hats, men in Bulgaria copy every fashion set by the *Knyaz*.'

'Did the wedding photograph reach your father in time?' I enquired solicitously.

'Yes, but only just. It meant that Papa died in peace. By the time Julia and I arrived here two weeks later he was with my mother in Paradise.'

Her face took on an ineffably sad look. She fidgeted with her enamel glove buttons. 'Up to now,' she continued, 'our subterfuge has worked. Undoubtedly it forestalled Konstantin's efforts to seize my lands.'

Tears started in her eyes. 'Now she is gone I am completely alone. Konstantin will redouble his efforts to wrest my lands from me.'

Her beautiful face was distorted with a spasm of despair.

My companion and I sat in silence for some little time after listening to this extraordinary narrative. Holmes rose to his feet. 'Madam, Dr. Watson and I may be able to do something about that. Let the weight of the matter rest upon us rather than you. We anticipate an appointment at the Palace very shortly.'

My spirits rose. When Holmes swoops, he swoops with the speed and certainty of the Indian kite-hawk.

He continued, in a gentler tone, 'Should you wish to marry an English cavalry officer I am sure Watson here will find you someone suitable and would be pleased to be the Best Man. It would necessitate your returning to our shores.'

'I shall bear that in mind, Mr. Holmes,' came her whispered reply.

CHAPTER XX
IN WHICH THE SWORD STICK IS TO PUT TO USE

THE Prince responded quickly to our request for a photographic session with Colonel Kalchoff. We were to return to the Palace at sun-up on the morrow with the bellows camera. Everything would be ready. Two Palace staff would meet us at the Red Staircase to carry the heavy photographic equipment to a suitable studio.

This time we were led down a long stone-flagged passage hung with orange and lemon-coloured tapestries to a small out-of-the-way monk-like cell at the back of the building, half-hidden by rhododendrons and creepers. The walls were busy with aquarelles of flowers and inset with fragments of Roman bas-reliefs. Above a profusion of bouquets of dried flowers in vases, there hung a large picture, clearly recently painted: a view of the Bosphorus, the Golden Horn, Saint Sophia, and the great wall of Constantinople. Floating in the glow of an apocalyptic sky was a splendid horseman, Ferdinand.

More prosaically dressed in a smock, the real Ferdinand stood at an easel by the window. He had surrounded himself with varnishing pots scattered across a beautiful Aubusson rug, a paint-brush in one hand, the Marquess of Salisbury's sword stick in the other. At our entry he stabbed the brush into a jar of cleaning fluid and turned to greet us. As he did so the doors behind us were flung open. Colonel Kalchoff strode in, dressed in the precise attire he had worn as Sherlock Holmes No. V, the fine mustachios gleaming, the Egyptian-blue cloak and its silk lining ablaze with colour. Words of greeting began to cross his lips.

'Konstantin,' the Prince interrupted in a business-like manner, 'while Dr. Watson is setting up the camera, I believe there is the small matter Mr. Holmes wishes to discuss with you.'

The Prince's tone turned to one of shocked indignation. 'An assassination—is that not so, Mr. Holmes?'

'I don't see—' Kalchoff began, a chill of fear springing to his eyes.

My companion stepped forward, his face dark. He stood in front of the War Minister with that quick, fierce gleam of his deep-set eyes before which many a criminal had cowered. He held up the wedding photograph.

'Colonel,' Holmes ordered, 'may I ask you to examine Captain Barrington's fine mustachios in this photograph?'

A deep silence ensued.

'But I see you do not need to examine them,' my comrade continued coldly. 'You are fully aware they are the very ones you are wearing.'

Without taking his eyes from the War Minister, Holmes addressed the Prince. 'Your Highness, they are identical in the minutest degree to this wedding photograph and to the Sargent painting which you commissioned a year later, so identical it is impossible they are not the same false pair. The only way the War Minister could have obtained them is straight from the cheeks of the young woman he murdered in the forest the morning of the Sherlock Holmes competition in the belief he was killing Captain Barrington.'

My companion went on in a harsh voice, 'In a desperate effort to save herself, the young woman pressed through the powerful hands gripping her throat and ripped the mustachios from her cheeks. By exposing her sex she hoped her killer would have mercy on her, but to no avail. The Colonel chose not to spare her life for fear of arrest and disgrace.'

With a violent movement Kalchoff swung away from Holmes. He darted a fearsome look at his master, his eyes as savage as a cornered wild beast.

In German he began, 'Ferdinand, you have allowed me to be tricked! Do they know I did it with your—'

Although Colonel Kalchoff was to live for another seven minutes these were to be the last words he ever spoke.

The Prince's hand swung up. 'Konstantin, my dearest friend,' he returned in English, slipping the blade of the sword stick from its sheath, 'I have yet to show you the gift Mr. Holmes and Dr. Watson brought from the Prime Minister of *England!*'

As he uttered the word 'England', with the precision of a matador delivering the *estocada*, the Prince thrust the blade deep into Kalchoff's throat. The Minister's head jerked back. A terrible convulsion passed over his face. He gagged violently. One hand came up to drag at the sword. Blood sprang from almost-severed fingers, spattering the flame-coloured lining of the cloak. His mouth burst open like a laughing skull, spurting out a further torrent of blood. His good hand dropped to fumble beneath the cloak.

To my amazement, rather than stepping forward to save the hapless Minister, Holmes brought his hunting crop hard down on the man's lowered hand. A half-cocked Apache pinfire cartridge revolver concealed beneath the cloak clattered to the floor. With no barrel, a set of foldover brass knuckles for a handgrip, and a folding knife mounted right underneath the revolver drum for use as a stabbing weapon, the Apache is probably the nastiest piece of work you can put in your pocket.

Indisputably it contained the folding knife which had drained the murdered woman of her life.

The Prince was observing me with a slight smile. He said, 'Doctor, you're not looking quite yourself. You seem to be taken aback. You were a little tardy in drawing your service revolver. Your comrade may just have saved all our lives. Konstantin is the finest proponent in all Europe with that pistol, not disregarding even the Parisian underworld.'

'But your Royal Highness, you can't just—' I castigated, waving towards his dying victim.

The War Minister was staggering backwards towards the door, staring in horror from the Prince to Holmes and me and back to the Prince. The once-glittering black eyes were losing their fire. Death moved across his face.

Ferdinand retorted, 'Oh but my dear Doctor, I venture to think I can. These are the Balkans. I am a Balkan Prince.'

He turned towards the dying man.

I have it word for word in my note-book that he addressed him as follows: 'Don't worry, Konstantin, my old friend, you shall have a state funeral. I shall personally lay a golden wreath at your grave, as I did at Tsar Alexander's. The same wreath in fact. I retrieved it for occasions like this.'

For a further few long-drawn-out seconds, Kalchoff's legs emulated a grisly Portuguese two-steps waltz. Then he collapsed. Coolly the Prince stepped towards him and pressed a hand on his heart. Assured he was dead, with one palm he held the corpse's face down while with the other hand he withdrew the blade and ran it across his smock. He turned to look up at me.

'Dr. Watson, it seems you are no longer keen to take my Minister's photograph?'

'Indeed not,' I exploded.

'You appear horrified a monarch should stoop to methods unworthy of the head of a gang of thieves. I ask you to remember the destiny of Europe rests on my shoulders. Were I afforded a greater amount of freedom and fewer grave responsibilities I might have let him live.' He stood up. 'It's a good idea to wear a painter's smock if you have to stick a sword in someone. Mr. Holmes, do thank the Prime Minister for his gift. Tell him I have already made excellent use of it.'

He turned again to the body and examined the pockets, drawing out the Black Pearl of the Borgias. He held it up to the light. 'Well I never!' he exclaimed with an ironic look. 'Then it's true. The Borgia pearl *does* bring bad luck to its owner. I must decide who shall have it next.'

Still badly shaken, I stammered, 'But I thought the Minister was among your greatest supporters? In our presence you described him to his face as your most loyal and constant friend and ally.'

'Sovereigns have peculiar responsibilities,' Ferdinand replied. 'I learnt at my dear mother's knee the advice offered to the Hapsburg Emperor Franz Joseph by his statesman Prince Felix von und zu Schwartzenberg.'

'Which was?' I asked.

'No autocrat can afford to be either grateful or humane. Certainly I know my action would be considered very shocking in one's private affairs, but it is quite something else in matters of State. The moment the interests of my principality become involved I have to recollect that I am the Prince Regnant of Bulgaria.'

He clapped his hands. A small gaggle of servants ran in. In a silence broken into solely by the sound of the deceased's scraping heels, the three of us stood staring at Kalchoff's body as they pulled him away, like mules dragging out a slain bull.

The following morning a copy of the Sofia English-language newspaper was pushed under our door. Holmes picked it up. I left my chair and studied it over his shoulder. Dramatic black strips outlined the front page.

The headline blared: A FURTHER ATTEMPT TO ASSASSINATE OUR BELOVED RULER FOILED. TRAGIC DEATH OF WAR MINISTER.

The article continued: 'Yesterday, in the heart of the Palace, in the former boudoir of our dearest departed Princess Marie-Louise, a vile attempt was made on the life of our beloved Prince Ferdinand of Saxe-Coburg-Gotha by a Ruthenian assassin armed with a Russian needle-gun. It took place while the *Knyaz* and War Minister Kalchoff were saying goodbye to the famous English consulting detective Sherlock Holmes and his diarist Dr. Watson. Realising at once the danger to the Prince, the faithful Minister threw himself at the attacker. For his bravery he suffered a mortal wound through the throat. The would-be assassin fled and has so far eluded capture. The *Knyaz* considers it his duty to render to the eminent deceased those honours which his services have merited: a national funeral.'

Holmes lowered the newspaper. With complete disregard to the dramatic reporting, he said, 'The note brought to Captain Barrington by the stable-boy arranged a rendezvous in a forest glade near an *obrok*, ostensibly to engage with the vampire rumoured to have moved into the region from Istria, hence Captain Barrington insisting he would be back before sun-up the next day.'

Holmes looked across at me to be certain I was following his train of thought. 'After all,' he added, 'unless speared in the heart with a wooden stake, vampires retreat to their lair by dawn. Kalchoff waited just short of the rendezvous point. He may have checked the horse's gallop with a tight rope. While the rider lay winded on the ground, he began to strangle him. If all had gone to plan, a day or two later the body would have been identified, the killing easily explicable as the result of a robbery. The husband's death would irretrievably weaken Mrs. Barrington's hold on her estates, lands which Kalchoff yearned to gain for himself. But imagine Kalchoff's amazement when he found he was murdering a woman.'

After a pause, Holmes added, 'It was indubitably Kalchoff who lured Captain Barrington to his death in the forest, but it is clear from the Minister's last words the timing of the murder was Ferdinand's.'

'I have a question, Holmes—' I began.

My comrade offered me an encouraging look.

'Namely?'

'How would Kalchoff be certain that Captain Barrington would carry with him the most important clue of all, the note decoying him to his death? Wasn't that a great risk? What if Barrington—Julia—had left it behind? The note would inevitably have led to the culprit.'

'That's why Kalchoff arranged the rendezvous at the *obrok*. It is unlikely a foreigner would know the exact location of such a shrine. The note contained precise directions, almost certainly accompanied by a sketch—you recall Mrs. Barrington saying her husband turned it this way and that—ensuring the victim would bring it with him.'

'I can see why Kalchoff would murder Captain Barrington— but why would the Prince become involved?'

'*Cui prodest?* Ferdinand's mother and the nation press Ferdinand hard to remarry. Several prospects of Royal lineage have said no to his proposals of marriage, aware life in Balkan royal circles is likely to be both brutal and short. If not of his own station, then from Bulgaria's Upper Crust. The Prince's unusual gift to Mrs. Barrington—a pair of diamond swallows for her hair, given to him by the Viennese actress Kathi Schratt, and to Schratt by the Emperor Franz Josef— I took it to be a sign of unrequited love. After the killing, Kalchoff could say nothing to prevent his master waiting a while, then marrying Mrs. Barrington and absorbing her vast lands for himself. Ferdinand immediately saw through the request for a photographic session. He understood I was about to unmask the one witness who could implicate the Prince himself. It became imperative to eliminate him.'

'Pretty gory stuff,' I said with feeling, 'thrusting the blade into his throat like that. Better a thrust through the heart—'

'Even those of us who are not medical realise a bodkin in the wind-pipe makes it difficult to finish the sentence,' Holmes broke in, drily. He looked at me quizzically.

'Do you recall the Minister telling you the Prince's favourite saying?'

'"Better to reign in Hell than to serve in Heaven".'

'I asked Penderel Moon if he had heard the words before.'

'And?'

'It's a quotation from *Paradise Lost*. Kalchoff knew he was supping with Satan. He would have been wiser to use a longer spoon.'

'And Sir Penderel?' I asked. 'Was he in on the Barringtons' masquerade?'

'Most likely,' came the reply. 'A man so assiduous in England's affairs will go far. We must have a word in Mycroft's ear. I foresee Moon becoming our Ambassador to St. Petersburg, even the Vatican.'

CHAPTER XXI
IN WHICH HOLMES SPRINGS FURTHER SURPRISES

IT was the morning of our departure. Our princely host assigned a chauffeur to drive us in the Royal Mercedes to the Danube ferry. I was like a horse smelling its home stables. In three or four days' time we would be back in Baker Street. We would look down at the bright glint of straw adrift across the street, sniffing the perfume of coffee, the savour of bacon and sausages. We would once again be enveloped in an endless rumble of commissariat wagons rattling like plague-carts, the soul of London, the great ground-bass of London awake, as the poetic American traveller Madox Hueffer put it to me.

I followed the hotel porter down with our boxes, reflecting on the rhythm of our cases, dimly discerning certain dominant harmonies. Each was a play in three acts, the first with the freshness of the first raindrops of the Monsoon, our dinner at Simpson's Grand Cigar Divan; the second dark, sumptuous and violent, the Prince's fairy-tale palace, the murder, the vampire-ridden forests of Mount Vitosh. Now we would take our bow and glide out silently, in the English fashion, like the calm of a great ocean following the storm.

At the Palace, we climbed the Red Staircase for the last time. Sir Penderel Moon was waiting in an ante-chamber. He greeted us warmly. 'Mr Holmes, and you too, Dr Watson, I must thank you both from the bottom of my heart over the Barrington matter. You have solved a despicable crime.'

'Will you be asking Her Majesty's Government to make a formal protest?' I enquired. 'The Prince seems to have been deeply implicated in Julia's murder. Regardless of her subterfuge, she was a British citizen.'

The Legate's cheery smile froze. 'Dr. Watson!' he returned with a horrified look. 'Would you grant Kalchoff in death his greatest wish in life—to drive the Prince into the arms of the Hun?' He shook his head vehemently. 'It is vital the matter is left to settle quietly and discreetly. In all Europe Great Britain has no ally, and it may be doubted if she even has a friend. We have no need to add more hatred. Her Majesty's Government intends to make no protestation regarding the murder.'

Realising how taken aback I was by his words, in a calmer but still-urgent tone he went on, 'You must forgive me. I am not here to wish you God-speed but to inform you that Downing Street begs you to tell nobody of these events. To make them public would deeply embarrass and undermine the Prince. Imagine your charge being laid before the Cabinets of the Great Powers. In common manhood they would feel obliged to take the matter up. It would set in motion a very active press-service throughout Europe and beyond. From an excess of pique, the Prince might well forge an alliance with the Kaiser and the Sublime Porte. The Balkans are poorly provided with roads and means of communications. The Bulgarian railway tracks would offer a most efficient link between the two Empires, to great military and commercial value. It would be gravely to the detriment of peace in our time.'

He shook his head. 'No! And again no! Singular chance put in your way a most whimsical problem. Its solution must be your only reward. Captain Barrington will disappear for ever, the case never resolved. He will become a Balkan legend, sighted on moonlight nights on the slopes of Mount Vitosh, an Englishman in full dress uniform, riding a great charger, bearing who knows what message from the nether regions. If you weaken Ferdinand by implying he condoned, even instigated the murder—above all, that the murdered husband of a woman long rumoured to be the object of desire by the *Knyaz* himself turned out to be female, a female whose wondrous mustachios were a deliberate copy of the Prince's—why, the whole of Europe would laugh themselves silly! Under the avalanche of mockery and scorn, the Russian Tsar may well seize the opportunity to send his armies across the Danube and replace Prince Ferdinand with a Grand Duke of his own choosing. Soon the summer grass will be growing fast, the Tsar's cavalry would grow fat on its way to burn the Palace to a cinder. Dr. Watson, you are a military man. Look in the direction of the Danube with a telescope. Even from here you will see a hundred heliographs and a thousand observation-balloons winking and glinting in the evening sky. Precisely how long could Ferdinand's light field-batteries hold out against five Divisions of Cossack irregulars, each mounted rifleman equipped with three of the most modern magazine-rifles, and backed by the heaviest field-guns yet built?'

The Legate stretched out his hands. 'To you both must accrue the satisfaction of knowing you have solved a despicable crime and that the perpetrator is dead. I repeat, for the sake of peace in our time, you must never repeat a word of this to anyone. Never.'

He broke off to stare hard at me. 'Dr. Watson, you can achieve great effect through your pen. You may rightly feel all Europe should ring with your comrade's name, that Mr. Holmes should be ankle-deep with congratulatory telegrams. May I have your—'

'I give you my word,' I conceded reluctantly.

'No reference to the matter at all, either spoken or in writing?'

'I have pledged my word.'

At that moment the Prince arrived.

Sir Penderel lowered his voice, 'Unless of course the fellow loses his throne.'

***

Ferdinand was beautifully attired in a shimmering gold tunic, black breeches, and a large black beret surmounted by a lightly jewelled gold aigrette. In his right hand he carried the sword stick like a baton. 'I designed this uniform myself,' he explained with a hint of self-mockery. 'I have given myself a promotion. Yes, Dr. Watson, we Balkan Princes can do that sort of thing. Enough of being just a General. As from today, I am the first Bulgarian Field Marshal in the history of the world.'

The four of us walked down the grand staircase towards our waiting vehicle.

'You will be safer crossing my country by road rather than rail,' Ferdinand said. 'The Bulgarian railways are heavily supported by assassins and spies without number wandering back and forth between Vienna and Stamboul like souls adrift in Dante's Inferno, *l sol tace*. My driver will take you to the ferry-boat and see you across the Danube in time to catch the Orient Express to Paris. My private carriages will again be at your disposal. Gentlemen, I cannot exaggerate the pleasure I have had from your presence in my country. I hope this will not be the last visit you make.' He added with a mischievous smile, 'I shall have to think up more plots to get you here.'

From slightly behind me, Holmes's hand came forward, stretching towards our host. It held a telegram. The Prince took the envelope, removed the slip of paper, and held it out in the sunlight to read. He looked at Holmes sharply, his eyes wide, as though a stab of fear was passing through him. Then, just as suddenly, his face broke into a grin of delight.

'Mr. Sherlock Holmes,' the Prince continued, thrusting the telegram back into my comrade's waiting hand, 'not for nothing are you known as the Baker Street Demon. Your skill has exceeded all that I have heard of it. You are indeed the master.'

Holmes returned the telegram to a pocket in his Poshteen Long Coat and acknowledged the compliment with a slight nod. We turned and stepped away. Even before we reached the vehicle the Prince bent his face into his hands, wracked by a burst of unstoppable laughter, then, regaining his full height and a solemn expression, he raised a hand in a military salute.

From the comfortable seats of our vehicle, I turned for one last sight of the bewitching palace. A bemused Sir Penderel was staring at the Prince. Ferdinand bent over again, shaking with compulsive laughter, waving the sword stick above his back. We turned a corner. The Prince and his Palace were lost to sight.

When the noise of the wind and the vehicle's motor made it impossible for our driver to hear my words I turned to my companion.

'Holmes, I am unable to contain my curiosity for a moment longer. What was that telegram all about?'

'It was merely a message from the Library of the British Museum.'

'A message from the Library of the British Museum?' I parroted in wonderment. 'And on what subject were you in touch with the British Museum?'

'The preservation of ancient parchments.'

His brevity exasperated me. 'Holmes, I insist on the detail! What did the Library say about the preservation of ancient parchments? Why should such information first seem to put the fear of God into the Prince and then make him nearly collapse with laughter?'

'It concerns the Codex.'

'Ah, the Codex, of course!' I responded with a chortle. 'I shall never forget the look on his face when he found it had been returned. The very name Sherlock Holmes must have—'

'It may not have been as great a surprise to Ferdinand as you imagine,' my comrade interrupted.

I swivelled to look directly at him.

'By which you mean—?'

'To judge from your expression, Watson, the Prince must truly be as consummate an actor as the Roman emperor Nero. You recall my axiom that misdeeds bear a family resemblance? That if you have the details of a thousand at your finger's end, it is odd if you are unable to unravel the thousand and first? What of the distant echo of *The Adventure of the Second Stain*? Tell me, according to the Prince, how long had the Codex been stored in that cave?'

'Almost from the day he took the throne.'

'So he informed us. How long has that been?'

'Twelve years.'

'Thirteen to be exact, since 1887,' Holmes replied. 'He has a superstitious aversion to the number thirteen, hence he used twelve. Nevertheless, even one year would have been out of the question, let alone a baker's dozen.'

'I don't follow you, Holmes.'

'He gave us four reasons for hiding the Codex in the cliff-caves, one supernatural, and three scientific. Do you recall the latter?'

'I have them written down,' I replied.

'There is some way to go before we reach the River Danube, perhaps you would be kind enough—?' He pointed to my Gladstone bag.

I pulled it to me and retrieved my note-book.

'So, Watson, my dear friend, the first—?'

'The air in the cave interior is absolutely clean and free of dust.'

'Good! And the second?'

'The cave interior shields the Codex from bright light.'

'Sunlight especially. Third?'

'The ambient temperature is quite low. It hardly varies a degree throughout the year.'

'Being?'

'A permanent 11 to 12 degrees Centigrade.'

'In our language that would be?'

'A little over 50 degrees Fahrenheit.'

'All in all, the caves would appear to be the perfect place to store so venerable a manuscript, don't you agree?'

'They would, Holmes,' I replied. 'So why—?'

'My dear fellow, there was one absolutely vital matter which our wily friend chose not to mention.'

'That being?'

Holmes withdrew the telegram from a pocket and handed it to me.

'Read it aloud,' he commanded. 'I congratulate you, Watson. It was you who gave me the clue.'

Deeply engaged by Holmes's complimentary remark, I began, "Preservation of ancient manuscripts. Fumigate and store in a dust-free environment. Low light and temperature levels are critical. Exposure to sunlight should be kept to the absolute minimum. As a rule of thumb, the lower and more consistent the temperature the better'.'

My eyebrows gathered in a frown. 'Well, Holmes, so far it seems—'

'Please read on, dear chap.'

I went on, "However, in the experience of the British Library the most critical requirement for conservation is low relative humidity, between a minimum of 30% and a maximum of 50%. This prevents the growth of fungi (mould and mildew). Relative humidities at the lower end of this range are preferable since deterioration takes place at a slower rate'.'

I looked up at my companion with a puzzled expression. 'Holmes, you said I gave you the clue—what clue?'

'Humidity,' Holmes repeated. 'The fourth ingredient. The most vital of them all. When we set off from Sofia the Prince told us the monks used to produce a special wine in the galleries of the caves. According to him, it closely resembled the wine produced in Champagne—do you recall his peroration on the wines of Bulgaria?'

'I do, yes,' I replied, 'but—'

'Anyone with the Prince's knowledge of alchemy is aware that high humidity is an essential part of producing such wines. Humidity over 75% for red wine and over 85% for the white is ideal for wine-ageing and barrel storage. You must recall the extreme humidity of the Baptistery?'

'It was very humid, certainly.'

'About 80%, I would estimate. Would you agree?'

'It was quite like the approach of the South Asia monsoon season, yes.'

'I have remarked on this before, Watson, that you have been of the most vital use to me in several of our cases, and again in this. I spotted how you sweated like a pig despite the modest temperature. It certainly suggests your Polka and Mazurka days are over, my dear fellow. No more quick-stepping to a Fife and Drum band, you must embrace the Waltz and the Two-Step. Even before we reached the Altar stone it seemed odd to me that a manuscript of such antiquity and mystical power would be left in such conditions. I realised at once it was never taken from its hiding-place BECAUSE IT WAS NEVER STORED

THERE. At most the Codex had been placed in the caves a matter of days, even hours, before our arrival.'

'But the Prince said he had sought the advice of the British Museum, the very source you—'

'Certainly he said that, though I suggest it was extremely unlikely, or at the very least we can say he didn't follow it,' Holmes replied laughing.

'Then why—?'

'Our friend needed to remove himself from the Capital while the murder of Captain Barrington took place. By dreaming up the theft of the Codex the Prince had a fine excuse to invite us to his country. By pretending the Codex had been stored in those far-off caves, he had reason to take us on a trip lasting at least three days.'

'He must have overlooked what a fine chemist you are, until you handed him the telegram. That's when he realised you had seen through the deception all along.'

'He realised it at once.'

'Which explains why he—'

'Scowled? Yes. His first thought must have been I was about to expose his trickery to the world. Within seconds it dawned upon him we must have been silenced. Why otherwise would I hand *him* the evidence which could indicate the disappearance of the Codex was part of a murderous plot? Why not simply put such information in the hands of Messrs. Reuter or the Balkan correspondent of the *Pall Mall Gazette* and let public uproar take its course? The Prince realised our own Government had hamstrung us. *That* was when he burst into laughter.'

Holmes shook his head with a glance of comic resignation and gave a chuckle. 'There never was, and never will be another Prince as foxy as Ferdinand. We must hope to encounter him again.'

I pondered on this unexpected revelation.

'Holmes,' I returned, 'that leads me to something which puzzles me still—even now there are matters still dark to me.'

'Ask on, my friend. I shall be your fellow prisoner for some hours in this contraption. You are very welcome to put any questions you like.'

'My first is, I am sure, a very minor one, Holmes, so please don't jump down my throat—when we left the Barrington villa after our first visit, you asked me if I had noted the presence of a tantalus containing brandy and whisky. I had not. Nor had I noted decanters of gins or vermouths and kirsches. Was the absence of spirits of especial importance?'

'The lack of a tantalus struck me as odd. It followed on the heels of my first observation, that Barrington's mustachios had changed not a jot between his marriage photo and the painting by Sargent a year later. I can see that a Captain in the Connaught Rangers could conceivably have settled into the life of a teetotaller upon marrying—I recall you giving up drink when you tied the knot with Miss Morstan—but surely he would not inflict his new-found temperance on every one of his guests? What of visits by officers of his old regiment? What choice words would *they* use in the face of an offer of a milky *Advokaats*?'

'How do you explain this oddity, Holmes?'

'Simply by deducing the Barringtons invited no-one to hobnob at their villa, particularly anyone who could discuss military affairs or might have served in Africa with the real Captain Barrington. You and I were allowed in only *in extremis*. And we can deduce neither Mrs. Barrington nor Julia touched alcohol themselves except for the *Advocaats*.'

I digested his words for some moments and continued, 'Holmes, I have a further question. When we were in the forest glade, you said that Julia's cold-blooded killer deserved the hangman's noose, that of the 40-odd murderers in your career so far—'

'—he, most emphatically of them all,' Holmes affirmed.

'Yet as soon as you deduced it was Colonel Kalchoff you invented a device to expose him in front of Ferdinand of all people—and in the Prince's private quarters. Why didn't you oblige Kalchoff to face a Court of Law? Who could possibly listen to your reasoning and have any doubts as to the man's guilt!'

'Where was our evidence? What violent enmity did he bear towards this murdered woman, a complete stranger to him and everyone else? Where was the note calling Barrington to the *obrok*? What of the monogrammed handkerchief he didn't drop?'

He gave a short, sardonic laugh. 'No, my friend, no gallows awaited him. Even an Old Bailey jury packed full of honest Englishmen would have set our Colonel free in the blink of an eye.'

It dawned upon me. I stared at my companion aghast.

'Holmes, are you saying you engineered the photographic session at the Palace solely to lure Kalchoff—'

'—to his death? Of course! It was a deliberate ambuscade, a private court-martial. How else would a great danger to England be removed? How else would the dead woman have been revenged? How else would Mrs. Barrington be freed of this cousin before he could take her lands—and probably her life? It was serendipity indeed when the Prince gave you the Sanderson camera. Kalchoff saw us flinging ourselves from the theatre. No more than a day would pass before he discovered our destination was not the midnight train to Paris but the body in the Mausoleum. From there it would be a matter of moments before he worked out that the one clue pointing towards the murderer lay with those mustachios, that his foolhardy use of them for the Sherlock Holmes competition now threatened his liberty, even his life.'

'Holmes,' I protested, 'surely you could not anticipate the Prince would stick a sword through Kalchoff's throat the moment you—'

'—proved the mustachios could only have been Julia's in her disguise as Captain Barrington? Not only did I foresee it, I depended upon it. Any delay in ending Kalchoff's life would have given him time to perpetrate some fresh atrocity. I smiled to myself when upon our entry I saw the Prince held the paint brush in one hand, the sword stick in the other. Our client knew that even he may not be safe from the War Minister's obsessive ambition once Kalchoff realised the Prince's intentions towards Mrs. Barrington.'

'But what of your maxim that justice must be done, that the depravity of the victim is no condonement in the eyes of the law?'

'My dear fellow,' Holmes replied calmly, 'once in a while we must make our plea to a higher, purer law. You recall your words upon the murder of Charles Augustus Milverton, "that it was no affair of ours; that justice had overtaken a villain", and my words which you quote so inimitably in the *Adventure of the Speckled Band* regarding Dr. Grimesby Roylott, that I cannot say his terrible death is likely to weigh very heavily upon my conscience?'

Not for the first time in our long career together I realised it was Holmes's contradictory nature, his Celtic insight that faith in reason cannot be absolute, which was and remains the engine propelling him so swiftly and inexorably along the path from mortal to myth.

My thoughts returned to the beautiful Bulgarian women we had left behind. None of us is the youngest we have ever been, I thought ruefully, but Holmes's unthinking offer of me as her next Best Man was a forcible reminder of my advancing years. What would happen to her now?

We came to a long straight stretch of road. The chauffeur reached to one side and passed back a bulky package wrapped in French serge. It contained a butcher-blue tunic, high collar with three stars, and a hat adorned with pale-green feathers, the ceremonial uniform of an Austrian cavalry general. Beneath the tunic lay black trousers with red stripes down the sides and a gold-braided Bauchband with tassels. A page of fine pink notepaper lay half tucked into a pocket. I could hear Foxy Ferdinand's voice as I read his words to my comrade-in-arms:

"'Dear Mr. Holmes, my tailor Hammond in the Place Vendôme created this uniform for your brother. When I am next in London I should like Mycroft to receive me in it at Victoria Station where he and I will pose for Dr. Watson and his camera. I have pinned to the tunic a new Order which I have just invented, the National Order of Military Merit, Grand Cross. Let me know if you would like me to invent a similar Order for you in recognition of your great service to my country in recovering the Codex Zographensis".'

There was a scrawled post-script. 'If not a military order, I am cultivating a new type of rose with four very pretty scarlet petals which I could name *Rosa sherlockholmesia*.'

This was followed by a Post-post-script: 'I forgot to inform you during your stay that His Imperial Majesty, The Sultan Abdülhamid II, Emperor of the Ottomans, Caliph of the Faithful (also known as The Crimson Sultan), wished you to travel on to an audience with him in the Sublime Porte, as he is a long-time admirer of your skill as a consulting detective.

Apologies for failing to pass his invitation on to you in time. It quite slipped my mind.'

Chapter XXII
WE CONTINUE OUR JOURNEY HOMEWARD

BY early evening we were comfortably reinstated in the Prince's magnificent carriages aboard the Orient Express tucking into Venison and Red Wine pie followed by Orange Crème Caramel with Cointreau oranges. After dinner Holmes laid out a box of matches in front of him and lit up a Dublin-clay pipe primed with an especially rank shag purchased in Sofia, thick blue cloud-wreaths spinning up from him. His eyes sparkled.

'Watson,' he reminisced, 'it is a pity you are not able to lay this most exotic case on the desk of your Editor. We shall console ourselves that the secret history of a nation is often so much more intimate and interesting than its public chronicles. Do you remember the unusual reception afforded us on our arrival at the Stone Wedding?'

'Of course!' I exclaimed.

'How will you look back on it?'

'It was the damnedest close-run thing. A few more yards and we'd have been blown to smithere—'

'A few more yards may have seen us killed, certainly,' my comrade interrupted, 'but it would have been entirely accidental.'

I stared at him. 'How do you mean?'

'It would not have been part of the script.'

'Perhaps you would be kind enough to explain? What script?'

'Do you recall Penderel Moon's words on the Prince's linguistic abilities?'

'I remember them exactly. I am a great admirer of anyone who speaks so many languages so fluently.'

'Remind me.'

'He said: "the Prince is the finest of linguists. With his mother and foreign diplomats he converses in brilliant French. He addresses the *Sobranje* in excellent Bulgarian. He boasts in perfect English and Italian. He swears in the coarsest Hungarian, Macedonian and Russian, and he employs his native German dialect with the servants he brought with him from the family seat in Coburg".'

'Superb, Watson! Tell me, despite the effect of the explosion on your ears, did you notice which of those languages he employed to shout at our attackers?'

'Only that it sounded guttural.'

'It was *Ostfränkisch*, a German dialect which I have studied. Why should such a polyglot use a tongue of his native land to shout at Russian or Macedonian assassins if he swears like a trooper in both their languages?'

'I have no idea, Holmes,' I responded. 'Why would such a polyglot do that?'

'He wouldn't.'

'Then—?'

'Our robust welcome at the Stone Wedding was a piece of theatre arranged entirely for our entertainment. The fact that the incompetence of the Palace staff nearly blew us to smithereens is another matter.'

'So what did he shout if it wasn't what he told us at the time—' I looked at the note-book '"—You Macedonian assassin scum, lackeys of the crazy people in St. Petersburg, run for your lives. I have here with me Sherlock Holmes and Dr. Watson!"?'

Holmes replied, 'His exact words were, "You bloody fools, you nearly killed Sherlock Holmes and Dr. Watson, let alone me! I'll have your arses for breakfast. I told you to detonate that stuff *after* the picnic, not now!".'

We laughed uproariously. I patted my pocket. In it lay the *Knyaz*'s Philadelphia Baby Derringer used by John Wilkes Booth in his assassination of Abraham Lincoln. It would go well in my small armoury with several other Baby Derringers, each sold as the very one employed to kill the American President on that terrible April night when I was just twelve years of age.

CHAPTER XXIII
AFTERWORD

A FEW weeks after their return from Bulgaria, a package addressed to Watson arrived at 221B Baker Street from Capri. It contained a magnificent cat's-eye and diamond tie-pin. A note in the Prince's hand accompanied the gift: 'To my great friend Dr. Watson, a small memento of your visit to my country. I am certain the blood of a Crusader runs in your veins. I feel that, should circumstances require it, you are quite capable of rising in your stirrups and dealing an infidel a blow with a mace which would cause him profound astonishment.' A separate card stated: 'This pin was purchased in Constantinople in 1890. Worn for 10 years by the Prince Regnant and future Tsar of Bulgaria.'

Accompanying it, for Holmes, was a scarlet shirt of the *Tirailleurs de la Garde*, 'In token of sincere regard—and to brighten up your wardrobe'.

Six months after Holmes and Watson returned to England an unsigned note in a woman's hand arrived at their Baker Street lodgings which read, 'It may please you to know the ashes of the young woman found dead on Mount Vitosh have been retrieved from their resting place in the Church of St. Louis at Philippopolis and reburied in a quiet and beautiful glade in the grounds of the Kalchoff estate.'

'Foxy' Ferdinand did eventually remarry, in February 1908. His bride was the Princess Eleonore Caroline Gasparine Louise Reuss zu Köstritz. She was considered "a plain but practical... capable and kind-hearted woman." It was another marriage of convenience and dynastic necessity.

In October 1908, Ferdinand proclaimed Bulgaria's *de jure* independence from the Ottoman Empire and titled himself

Tsar. A few years later he made a rare but grave error of judgment by taking his adoptive country into the Great War on the side of Kaiser Wilhelm. In 1918, by now a widower again, Ferdinand left Bulgaria for luxurious exile in Coburg for the final thirty years of his remarkable life. The ex-Tsar of Bulgaria died peacefully in his sleep during the night of September 10th 1948, at the age of eighty-seven. His surviving children, daughters Eudoxia and Nadezhda, were at his bedside. Heaven's gift to the political cartoonists of Europe from his accession to the Bulgarian throne in 1887 to his fall in 1918 was no more.

Sir Penderel Moon remained for a while as British Legate to Bulgaria. On his departure from Sofia he received an official despatch from Sir Edward Grey, as follows:

'I desire to take this opportunity to convey to you the high appreciation entertained by His Majesty's Government of the manner in which you have filled the post of British representative at Sofia. Your interesting and able reports on the situation proved invaluable to His Majesty's Government in their efforts for the maintenance of peace, and the moderating influences which you successfully exerted.'

Ten years after the events portrayed, Sir Penderel Moon, now honoured with the Most Distinguished Order of (military saints) Michael and George, was appointed British Ambassador to the great white Capital St. Petersburg. He was ambassador at the time of the Russian Revolution in 1917.

His autobiography titled *My Mission to Bulgaria Recollected at Leisure* was published in 1923.

ACKNOWLEDGEMENTS

Arthur Conan Doyle, creator of Sherlock Holmes and Dr. Watson. To help reflect the atmosphere of those faraway days I have here and there taken favourite words and phrasing straight from the canon.

The superb historian Judith Rowbotham at Nottingham Trent University whose researches on Victorian and Edwardian crime and its historical context offer detective-fiction writers wonderful tools of the trade. I particular appreciate the attention to detail in going through the several re-writes of *the Bulgarian Codex* and making suggestions, most of which I took up.

Alun Hill FCIJ for running a sharp eye over both text and layout.

Ditto Ann Leander, formerly of the Bangkok Writers group, for running a further eye over the text and making valuable suggestions.

And Robert and Aileen Ribeiro, for going through with such a knowledgeable eye (as befits the owners of the house built by famous Holmes and Watson illustrator Walter Paget) as they did earlier with *Sherlock Holmes And The Dead Boer At Scotney Castle* (MX Publishing 2012).

Andrew (Андрей) in faraway Russia for mapping Holmes's and Watson's journeys to and within Bulgaria. (There are plans to translate *the Bulgarian Codex* into Russian)

Dim & Distant Rare and Second-hand Bookshop. Heathfield, East Sussex TN21 8HU. Dave Berry's hidden treasure of a bookshop. Don't miss the chance to pick and choose wonderful books, including bargains outside the shop. A sister store opened in Eastbourne Summer 2012.

And to the following for their valuable research assistance:

V&A Theatre & Performance Enquiry Service, a superb, friendly resource on matters Victorian and Edwardian. For example, 'We have checked our archives and relevant reference works and the earliest evidence we can trace of Vesta Tilley performing as a soldier is during World War One. In particular, she had two characters - 'Tommy in the Trench' and 'Jack Tar Home from Sea' - which formed part of her recruitment drive. This was accompanied by singing suitable topical songs such as The Army of Today's Alright , Jolly Good Luck to the Girl Who Marries a Soldier , and In Dear Old England's Name. She visited hospitals and sold War Bonds, as well as encouraging men at her shows to enlist (during the early part of the war before conscription was put in place).'

Dr Michael Pritchard FRPS, Director-General, The Royal Photographic Society, for technical advice on the advances in cameras and photography in the late-19th and early-20th Centuries, viz 'When abroad, Watson, being a doctor and probably a keen amateur photographer, would most likely have developed his plate in his hotel room and then made a contact photograph from it which he would have sent to the *Strand* by post, or perhaps had a fellow traveller hand-carry it back to London.'

Jeff Sobel, son of Eli Sobel, my favourite Dean of Honours at UCLA, for technical advice on contemporary weaponry, especially the very unpleasant Apache revolver.

For friendly and encouraging reviews of my recent novel, *Sherlock Holmes And The Dead Boer At Scotney Castle*:

Felicia Carparelli in faraway Chicago, who writes under the pseudonym 'maurice chevalier' (quote: *the Dead Boer* contains 'Lots of action and plot devices and a villain who Holmes says rivals Moriarty. This is a healthy Sherlock pastiche with many commendable elements.')

Ditto Britain's former Foreign Secretary, Sir Malcolm Rifkind who emailed, 'Dear Tim Symonds, just to say that I have just finished reading *The Dead Boer at Scotney Castle*. I greatly enjoyed it and found it a great yarn! It kept one guessing right to the end which all good crime novels should do. Sherlock Holmes (and Conan Doyle) would have been impressed!'

And to Tracey Snape for her review of *the Dead Boer* in the Association of British Investigators Journal ('cleverly written in the style of Conan Doyle' and 'well worth a read for lovers of the inventive art of detection').

Google and Amazon and Wikipedia for all the research I needed at my very fingertips even seated on logs in the ancient woods of East Sussex.

Last and certainly not least, my partner Lesley Abdela for her happy involvement in both *the Dead Boer* and *the Bulgarian Codex*, and her wonderful journalist's eye on my plots.

SELECT BIBLIOGRAPHY OF WORKS CONSULTED

In addition to the several Conan Doyle stories mentioned in the Adventure—:

Buchanan, George, *My Mission to Russia, and Other Diplomatic Memories*, (Vol I), (Cassell, 1923)

Buchanan, Meriel, *Ambassador's Daughter*, (Cassell, 1958)

Constant, Stephen, *Foxy Ferdinand, Tsar of Bulgaria*, (Franklin Watts, 1980)

Haslip, Joan, *The Emperor and The Actress: the love story of Emperor Franz Josef and Katarina Schratt*, (Weidenfeld & Nicolson, 1982)

Cloete, Stuart, *A Victorian Son: an autobiography 1897-1922*, (Collins 1972)

Poiret, Paul, *My First Fifty Years*, (Victor Gollancz. 1931)

Jezernik, Božidar, *Wild Europe: the Balkans in the Gaze of Western Travellers*, (Saqi Books, 2003)

Upward, Allen, *The Prince of Balkistan*, (Chatto & Windus, 1895). A novel of international intrigue set in a mythical Balkan state very much like *fin de siècle* Bulgaria.

also

Dickson Carr, John, *The Life Of Sir Arthur Conan Doyle*. (Carroll & Graf, 1949)

Lycett, Andrew, *Conan Doyle, the Man who created Sherlock Holmes*, (Phoenix, 2008)

GLOSSARY

Those who have read *Sherlock Holmes And The Dead Boer At Scotney Castle*, and now *Sherlock Holmes And The Case of The Bulgarian Codex* will note that Watson gets a better deal than he does in the original canon or in most television and motion picture portrayals. Though not gifted with Holmes's sharp intellect, Watson has a good intelligence and many excellent qualities which should be burnished like the brass on his old Regimental uniform. Words written later by an editor describing the Crime writer John Carr could equally have applied to the fictional Dr. John H. Watson: 'All his instincts were for a less scientific world, a less mechanised one, a more romantic one…he would have been happier in the 18th Century, with sword play and sudden personal dramas, with costumes and carriages, and beaus and belles, with long talks over mugs of wine near the fireplace, and if any crimes had been committed, they were fashionably done, with éclat'.

Watson is brave, honourable, loyal, unshakeable in pursuit of justice, an immediate and deep admirer of women. The actions of a man falling in love are never far from comedy. Every so often Conan Doyle seemed tempted to offer his character schoolboy infatuations, as I have here with Mrs. Barrington, alas, far too young for him in Victorian or Edwardian England. Best Man at her future wedding, courtesy of Holmes, is all I could offer him.

Watson puts up with Holmes's put-downs with good grace, although they sting. He thinks hard about life. The fact he has so many friends ever ready to meet him at one of his several watering-holes like The Guards or the Punjab Club indicates he is an engaging presence and a man of the world.

Orient Express: The Orient Express is the name of a long-distance passenger train service originally operated by the *Compagnie Internationale des Wagons-Lits*. It ran from 1883 to 2009 and is not to be confused with the Venice-Simplon Orient Express train service, which continues to run.

The two city names most prominently associated with the Orient Express are Paris and Constantinople (Istanbul), the original endpoints of the timetabled service.

'Swamp adder': this appears in Conan Doyle's *The Adventure of the Speckled Band*. The (mythical) dangerous creature is said to be yellow with brown speckles and to slither around in India.

A Scandal in Bohemia: this was the first of Watson's chronicles to be published in the *Strand* and is one with no dead bodies. While the currently married Dr. Watson is paying Holmes a visit, the great detective is called upon by a masked gentleman introducing himself as Count Von Kramm, an agent for a wealthy client. Holmes quickly deduced he is in fact Wilhelm Gottsreich Sigismond von Ormstein, Grand Duke of Cassel-Felstein and the hereditary King of Bohemia. The King admits this, tearing off his mask. The King is to become engaged to a young Scandinavian princess but his in-laws-to-be would certainly not agree to the marriage if any evidence of his former liaison with an American opera singer, Irene Adler, was passed to them. A well-known adventuress, Adler is threatening to reveal the relationship upon the announcement of the King's betrothal by sending a photograph of the King (then the Crown Prince) and Adler together to the newspapers.

The Diogenes Club: this is a fictional gentleman's club co-founded by Sherlock's older brother, Mycroft Holmes. It features in several Sherlock Holmes stories, most notably 'The Greek Interpreter'. It seems to have been named after Diogenes the Cynic (although this is never explained in the original stories). It is described as a place where men can go to read without any distractions, and as such the number one rule is that there is no talking, to the point where club members can be excluded for coughing.

Kaldrmi: cobbled roadway.

Pennsylvania Limited: the Pennsylvania Railroad was an American Class I railroad founded in 1846. Commonly referred to as the "Pennsy", it was for decades the largest railroad in the world, with 6,000 miles of track, and famous for steady financial dividends, high quality construction, constantly improving equipment, technological advances (such as replacing wood with coal), and innovation in management techniques for a large complex organisation.

The Adventure of the Blue Carbuncle: the intriguing story of what was to be found in the crop of a Christmas goose. The seventh in *The Adventures of Sherlock Holmes*.

The Adventure of the Copper Beeches: the attempt by Mr. Rucastle to prevent his daughter marrying her sweetheart by getting a young woman resembling her to be visible in his house, while his daughter is locked away. Holmes frees her. The last of twelve in *The Adventures of Sherlock Holmes.*

The Adventure of the Bruce-Partington Plans: secret submarine plans are missing. One of eight stories in the cycle collected as *His Last Bow*, the second and final appearance of Mycroft Holmes.

10 Downing Street: this is still the official residence of the British Prime Minister while holding the office. At the time of *The Case of The Bulgarian Codex* the Prime Minister, the third Marquess of Salisbury, took a particular interest in foreign affairs. He died in 1903 and was buried in Westminster Abbey in an altar tomb of black marble with a bronze effigy.

Poshteen Long Coat: (also 'Posteen') was an Afghan outer garment often worn by officers for warmth in low temperatures, in Sikh Brigades etc. Can be made from fur, leather or sheepskin.

The Watson Codex: this is a fictional treatise on *rigor mortis* and an important element in Holmes's solution to the crime in *Sherlock Holmes And The Dead Boer At Scotney Castle* (MX Publishing 2012).

Sarus Crane: this is the tallest crane species and tallest of all flying birds, with a height of about 176 cm. The adult male has pale grey plumage.

Yataghan: this is a type of Ottoman knife or short sabre in general use from the mid-sixteenth to late nineteenth centuries.

Chapeau de haute forme: top hat.

fée verte: translates as 'green fairy' and was the colloquial French term for absinthe, an anise-flavoured spirit derived from botanicals, including the flowers and leaves of *Artemisia absinthium* (a.k.a. 'grand wormwood'), together with green anise, sweet fennel, and other medicinal and culinary herbs. Absinthe originated in the canton of Neuchâtel in Switzerland in the late eighteenth century. For decades from 1915 it was considered so dangerous a potion the French passed a law forbidding its sale.

Ortolan: a bird in the bunting family. It was sometimes consumed drowned in armagnac, plucked, and stripped of its feet and a few other tiny parts.

Pinkerton Agency: the famous American detective agency established by Allan Pinkerton in 1850, which was at its height in the last decades of the nineteenth century up to 1914, the largest private detective agency in the world. Conan Doyle knew William Pinkerton, and his final Holmes novel, *Valley of Fear* (1915), was based on the exploits of a Pinkerton detective

The Adventure of the Reigate Puzzle: published as *The Adventure of the Reigate Squire*, and one of the twelve stories in *The Memoirs of Sherlock Holmes*, it was among Conan Doyle's favourite Holmes stories, dealing with the murder of a coachman who turns out to have tried to be a blackmailer. Holmes uncovers the two local squires who are the perpetrators.

The Adventure of the Beryl Coronet: this was the eleventh story in *The Adventures of Sherlock Holmes*, and features the attempted theft of the beryl coronet, a family heirloom left as security for a loan. Holmes solves the mystery of the real attempted burglar from clues such as footprints in the snow.

Ribston-pippin: Also known as 'The Glory Of York'. A small aromatic apple possibly grown from one of three apple pips sent from Rouen, Normandy, in 1708 to Sir Henry Goodricke of

Ribston Hall at Knaresborough, Yorkshire. Ribston is one of the possible parents of the Cox's Orange Pippin.

The Adventure of the Six Napoleons. One of 13 stories in the cycle collected as *The Return of Sherlock Holmes*. Set in 1900, Inspector Lestrade of Scotland Yard brings Holmes a seemingly trivial problem about a man wandering about London shattering cheap plaster busts of Napoleon Bonaparte.

The Adventure of the Speckled Band: one of four Sherlock Holmes stories classified as 'a locked room' mystery. First published in the *Strand Magazine* in February 1892, with illustrations by Sidney Paget and published as *'The Spotted Band'* in *New York World* in August 1905. Doyle later stated this was his best Holmes story.

The Red-Headed League: the story involved a newspaper want-ad offering work solely to gloriously red-headed male applicants. It first appeared in the *Strand Magazine* in August 1891, with illustrations by Sidney Paget. Conan Doyle ranked it second in his own list of twelve favourite Holmes stories.

Fauteuil: a style of open-arm chair with a primarily exposed wooden frame originating in France in the early eighteenth century.

Dolly Varden: character in Dickens's *Barnaby Rudge*, known for her colourful attire, large hats and flirtatious attitudes.

Apotropaics: Apotropaic magic (from Greek *apotrepein*, to ward off: *apo-*, away + *trepein*, to turn) is a type of magic intended to 'turn away' harm or evil influences, as in deflecting misfortune or averting the evil eye. Doorways and windows of buildings were felt to be particularly vulnerable to evil.

Salomé, **Oscar Wilde:** originally written in 1891, in French and translated into English in 1894. Plans for a performance in 1892 were halted as the Lord Chamberlain banned it (it was illegal to depict Biblical characters on stage). It was premiered (in French) in Paris in 1896, when Wilde was in Reading Gaol and then its next public performance was in Berlin in 1903. The first known performance in England, in English, was a private one, in 1905. Wilde used the form Iokanaan for John the Baptist.

Crape: The spelling 'crape' is the anglicised versions of the French crêpe, the silk or wool fabric of a gauzy texture, having a peculiar crisp or crimpy appearance.

I sol tace: translates as 'Where the sun is silent.' The Prince was very widely read.

C*ui prodest?* To whose benefit?

The Adventure of the Second Stain: Britain's Prime Minister Lord Bellinger and Trelawney Hope, the Secretary of State for European Affairs, come to Holmes in the matter of a document stolen from Hope's dispatch box, which he kept at home in Whitehall Terrace when not at work. If divulged, this document would bring about very dire consequences for all Europe, even war.

The Adventure of Charles Augustus Milverton: in this, Holmes refers to the death of the eponymous blackmailer. Holmes deliberately fails to reveal the identity of the woman who shot Milverton.

In 1905 Ford Madox Hueffer published his travellers' book on London titled 'The Soul Of London'.

****

Author's post-script: I realise when writing my Sherlock Holmes novels how much I owe my paternal grandfather for whatever insight I have into the Victorian/Edwardian period in which Holmes and Watson operated. My Bristol-born grandfather called himself Professor Mark James Burgess and throughout my early years transported my grandmother, my mother and me around the watering holes of England and the Channel Islands with his brass plate, setting up during the season as a Consultant Psychologist. He had all the paraphernalia of the Victorians including a handsome china phrenological head by L.N. Fowler which could now only be found at great expense in antique shops, and a beautiful teak and brass contraption which delivered a very high voltage to the brain for people suffering depression which practitioners of those times used without any medical qualifications whatsoever.

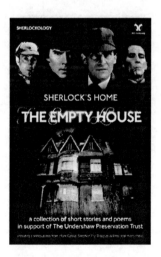

Also from MX Publishing

Sherlock Holmes Travel Guides

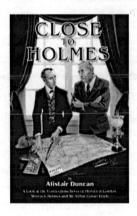 

And in ebook (stunning on the iPad) an interactive guide

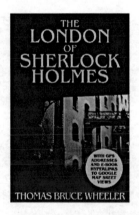

400 locations linked to Google Street View.

Also from MX Publishing

Biographies of Arthur Conan Doyle

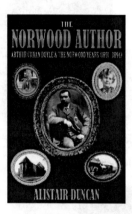 

The Norwood Author. Winner of the 2011 Howlett Literary Award (Sherlock Holmes Book of the year) and the most important historical Holmes book of 2012 'An Entirely New Country'.

Also from MX Publishing

 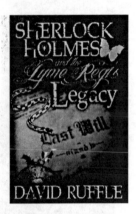

Sherlock Holmes and The Lyme Regis Horror and the sequel
Sherlock Holmes and The Lyme Regis Legacy

Sherlock Holmes – Tales from the Stranger's Room
An eclectic collection of writings from twenty Holmes writers.
Volume 2 now also available

www.mxpublishing.com

Also from MX Publishing

Sherlock Holmes Travel Guides

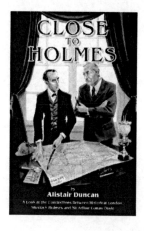 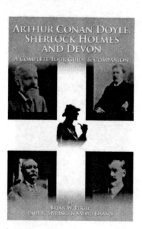

London Devon

In ebook (stunning on the iPad) an interactive guide to London

400 locations linked to Google Street View.

www.mxpublishing.com

Also from MX Publishing

Sherlock Holmes Fiction

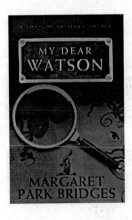 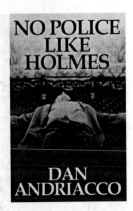

Short fiction (Russian Chessboard), modern novels (No Police Like Holmes), a female Sherlock Holmes (My Dear Watson) and the adventures of Mrs Watson (Sign of Fear, and Study in Crimson).

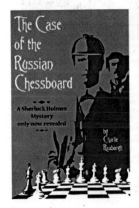  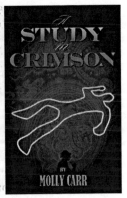

Also from MX Publishing

Biographies of Arthur Conan Doyle

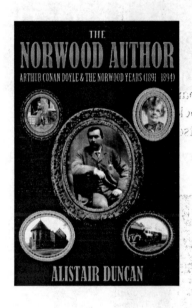

The Norwood Author. Winner of the 2011 Howlett Literary Award (Sherlock Holmes Book of the year) and the most important historical Holmes book of this year 'An Entirely New Country'

Also from MX Publishing

Cross over fiction featuring great villans from history

and military history Holmes thrillers

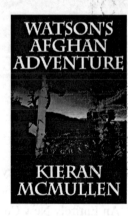 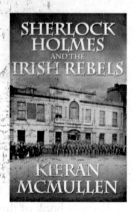

Also from MX Publishing

Fantasy Sherlock Holmes

And epic novels

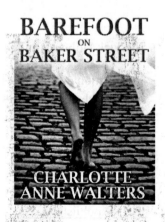

Lightning Source UK Ltd.
Milton Keynes UK
UKOW030136230413

209606UK00006B/205/P